Promise Kept.....I Remembered You

Written by:

Susan Centofanti Baricko

1

Dedication

This book is dedicated to two innocent young boys, now men, who had an important part in this story. At the time, they were not aware of everything that was going on around them, but they were certainly a highlight in my life. This is also dedicated to the son who was lost and never had the opportunity to live his life. I have never forgotten any of you and cherish the memories of those days gone by. Know that I will forever hold those memories in my heart.

Table of Contents

Prologue

This is the story of a young girl who was born in Petersville, New York in 1954. Suzie's parents were worlds apart on how to raise children and this would cause many conflicting messages for her and her younger brother, Joe. Her father was outgoing, friendly and loved to laugh. Her mother was more introverted, quiet, and found it difficult to laugh. Besides her brother Joe, Suzie had a large extended family that she absolutely adored. There were grandparents, aunts, uncles, cousins, and very close family friends around all the time and her childhood, barring the parental conflicts, was filled with love and happy memories.

As Suzie grew older, it was evident that she was much like her father. They shared many of the same ideologies, love of sports, and a fearlessness that was inborn. Her mother had envisioned a little girl in crinoline and lace, but that was certainly not Suzie. She climbed trees, played football with the neighborhood boys, built forts, and generally did things that were considered outside of the box. This would cause many unhappy moments between Suzie and her mother. Suzie could not even remember a time when her mother told her that she loved her which was always unsettling to her especially after her younger brother Joe was born. It was obvious, at least to Suzie, that her mother preferred Joe to her.

As Suzie approached the teen years, it was observed that her father trusted her to make good decisions when not around him. Her mother on the other hand was constantly suspicious of everything Suzie did or wanted to do. It was at the beginning of her middle school years that things worsened significantly when her mother started to refer to her as a whore, all because of the way she dressed.

Suzie would figure out that her mother treated her badly when she was frustrated or mad at her father, which seemed to be pretty often, all because she was more like her father than what her mother thought she should be. Suzie often sought solace with her grandparents. Suzie would learn that her mother was the way she was because of the childhood she had experienced and not having a positive role-model as a mother. There was just a lot of turmoil in this young girl's life and this did not help her to make the decisions she would ultimately make and change the course of her life forever.

Chapter 1

It was 1968 when innocent times were becoming tumultuous. It seemed to Suzie that her whole world was about to unravel as her parents, Jim and Carol, made a decision that would forever change her life. Suzie had been an exceptional student in school, excelling in academics and enrolled in a special program that catered to those beyond gifted. Had she been able to continue in this program it would have offered her a complete college education, finalizing with a position as a biological researcher for the foundation that was sponsoring this program in her home town of Petersville, New York. Suzie had been interested in biology since she monitored and recorded the metamorphosis of a caterpillar to butterfly as a young child. She focused on that and was determined to learn all she could and someday find the cure for cancer. We all have dreams.

Everything changed in 1968. Martin Luther King, Jr. was assassinated and the world seemed to turn inside out. Petersville experienced rioting as much of the country had. School buses had been over-turned, stores looted, and general chaos penetrated the once sleepy town. Jim and Carol decided that it was time to leave and move further north in an attempt to escape the down-slide of Petersville. There was also another reason that decision was made. Jim had been having an affair with a woman and Carol knew. She thought if they moved, it would make things better. Jim wanted to move because if they were out of town, it would be easier for him to continue to see his girlfriend without getting caught.

Unfortunately for Suzie, this move would take her away from the friends she had known since early childhood and all of the extended family that lived in that area. Family had always been important. There had been Sunday picnics and dinners at various family members' homes all her life and that was about to change. This was going to be a difficult time and Suzie started to feel isolated especially since Carol was not the most loving of mothers. Suzie had constantly been criticized even though she rarely did anything wrong. When she started middle school, Carol became nastier and was constantly calling her a whore just because of the way she dressed and the makeup she wore which was nothing outlandish, the style of the day. This criticism became an almost every day occurrence and Suzie just started taking it in stride, not even reacting to it any longer. She could not even remember her mother telling her that she loved her.

The move to Martin's Cove took place in the late summer between Suzie's eighth and ninth grade school years. This is a difficult time to make a change in any child's life. While visiting the new school and discussing class option with the guidance counselor, it was evident that this school did not offer any classes that could challenge Suzie and he suggested it would be in her best interest to send her back to Petersville to finish school but of course, Carol would not hear of this. The highest level of classes available were assigned and Suzie made a serious attempt to fit in, make friends, and adjust to the differences. Compared to what she had been used to, she thought this was a joke. She finished freshman year never studying and managed straight A's. At the beginning of sophomore year in Biology, she thought that they would be doing dissections and experiments like she had done in her previous school. That was not the case so Suzie went to the guidance counselor and had her schedule changed to all business classes. She also told him at that time, that she would take her junior year English in summer school so she could graduate a year early. Her new found friend, Kim, was planning on doing the same thing. The counselor was not happy with this idea and tried to discourage her, but that is exactly what Kim and Suzie would do.

Most of the kids her age were either immature or involved with drugs, something Suzie had a hard time understanding. In Petersville, the kids had been more mature and drugs were not something Suzie or her friends ever thought of doing. They were just too busy with other things and the town had offered different activities to keep their youth busy. In Petersville, they were able to walk downtown to the movies, for a pizza, to shop or just hang out. You could not do that in Martin's Cove. You needed a car to take you anywhere you wanted to go, and it was boring.

Suzie started hanging around with people that were older than her, Kim had a cousin who could drive and they often skipped school to just hang out.

When Suzie turned 16, she secured a job in one of the local drug stores which had an extensive make-up counter. The woman in charge of that part of the store was Jean. Jean had been a Rockette in New York City and started teaching Suzie how to do stage make-up because they offered a make-over service. She also worked behind the pharmacy counters with the owners, the pharmacists, and that was fun because of her interest in anything medical. She loved her job even when she had to work at the front counter as a cashier which included keeping the cigarettes and candy stocked. It gave her the opportunity to meet new people and Jean soon became a very important person in her life, she enjoyed all whom she worked with. It was a very good job for a young girl.

Chapter 2

As her junior year drew to a close, some of the friends she had made were graduating. Most of these people lived in the same lake community of Martins Cove as she did and there was a party at the lake one night. Suzie had acquired a 1965 Mustang which was her pride and joy; but, she chose to walk to the lake that night since it was not far. When Suzie arrived at the party, there were a lot of people there, most of them she knew, but there was a group of older guys whom she did not know. They worked with some of the people she knew building houses in the new development close by. Joining the party, she mingled with those she knew and was introduced to those she had not been acquainted with. They were sitting at a picnic table so she joined in their conversation, and also joined them when offered a drink. Conversation and laughter caused the time to go quickly when suddenly she realized that most of the people she knew had left. This was a bit awkward because she had to walk home alone.

She decided to leave and as she did one of the guys grabbed her hand. She asked what they were doing and they just laughed. Two of them held her down on the picnic table as the third one raped her. They took turns and when they were done they simply left, leaving Suzie lying on the picnic table with her eyes closed tightly and tears running down her face. When she tried to move, she felt the pain from being violated and just stayed on the table for a while. She didn't know what to feel, how to feel or what to do, but when she looked down and noticed how disheveled she looked she had to do something. She went in the lake and swam for a while. The cool water served to wash away the bloody evidence of what had happened and give her an excuse for the way she looked. Emerging from the lake, she went back to the picnic table and just sat there staring at nothing.

She did not know what to do as a flood of emotions coursed through her. She knew she couldn't tell her father, he had an Italian temper and could certainly kill them if he could find them. She couldn't tell her mother since all she did was refer to her as a "whore", that would only convince her that Suzie was one. She couldn't tell the police because in those days it was always the girls fault and Suzie had done nothing but go to a party and meet some new people. She walked home in a daze arriving a little after eleven. Her father was waiting up for her and said that it looked as if she had a good time, she quietly told him that she had. She took a shower, crawled into bed and cried herself to sleep vowing to never tell anyone what had happened and thinking about the fact that she would never have the opportunity to say 'no'.

Suzie became very distant and quiet. She had previously been more outgoing and enjoyed doing unusual things like working on cars, racing cars and just being a goofy kid of 16. The change was noticed by her father who figured that something had caused this change in his daughter, but every time he inquired she just told him that she wanted to go back to Petersville, to everything that was once safe and familiar. By that answer, he knew something more profound had occurred but left it alone deciding to keep a close eye on her. Any time he tried to get her to talk, she just withdrew even more. The worst part, was she no longer trusted anyone, including herself.

Summer school was about to begin, Suzie and Kim became closer, the best of friends. Usually best friends shared everything but Suzie did not tell Kim what had happened that night and never would. She blamed the change in her demeanor on the fact that things at home were not going well, Jim and Carol were fighting again as they had done in Petersville. When that happened, Carol treated her worse than ever but this was something she had become used to so she would just think, here we go again. Even at this young age Suzie figured out that she was so much like her father that Carol would take it out on her when she was frustrated or mad. The more Carol and Jim fought, the worse things got for Suzie and since she was pretty emotionless anyway, she just ignored it.

Work, school and Kim proved to be good outlets. Jean continued to teach Suzie about make-up and she had retained a few of her own clients that would come in for make-overs for special occasions. Jean was great and with the exception of telling her about the rape, she shared many other things with her. Jean was her 'go to' person. She was understanding and had a way of making Suzie feel worthy. About two weeks after the rape, she did tell Jean what had happened to her and Jean was devastated. After convincing Suzie to see a doctor, Jean accompanied her to the appointment just to make sure everything was fine. It was then that Suzie started taking birth control pills, she could not imagine getting pregnant in that way if it were to ever happen again. She was having a difficult time processing what had happened to her, remained distant, introverted, completely unsure of anything, and her self-esteem was not very good either.

Chapter 3

Suzie was scheduled to work one Saturday until six in the evening and with no scheduled make-overs her tasks were to be the cashier which entailed keeping the cigarettes and candy counters cleaned and stocked. She was filling the cigarettes when she turned around to get another carton of cigarettes, and there he was, 'Adonis' standing there watching her with a smile on his face that seared straight to her soul. With the voice of a God, he said, "What did you say your phone number was?" It took a second for her to compose herself and get her heart beating again when she managed to smile and very quietly gave him her phone number. He told her that his name was Sam, she told him her name was Sue, and he said that he already knew her name. Oh my, this extremely handsome man was paying attention to her and causing her to become quite uncomfortable. He promised to call her later and with that he was gone. It took her a minute to recover, process what had just happened and to continue with her responsibilities although her heart continued to pound as she tried to catch her breath.

She wanted to day to end so she could go home to get his phone call but it seemed that time just stood still. Negative thoughts crept into her head, thoughts that she often had lately. Would he understand, would he blame her, would she really have to tell him? Getting upset, she convinced herself that she should just ignore him and forget she ever met him. She was also convinced that he wouldn't be interested if he ever found out what had happened to her and that would be inevitable. Dating was not something that interested her anyway, she simply did not trust anyone. Finally, the store closed and she could go home. While driving, she convinced herself that she would just tell him she wasn't interested, he would not want her anyway if and when he ever learned what had happened to her. When she arrived home, she ate some dinner that had been saved for her, took a shower, and went to her room to record the day in her diary.

The phone rang, her heart skipped a beat when her father came to her door telling her she had a phone call and it was some guy. She would take the call in Jim and Carol's room which offered a bit of privacy. She sat down on the floor between their beds and picked up the phone. When she heard her father hang up the kitchen phone she said 'hello' and once again, his voice embedded itself in her soul.

The first thing he told her was that her name did not fit her and asked if it would be alright if he called her "Suzie." She never really cared for that name, but the way he said it sounded like music to her ears so she told him that was fine. He wanted her to call him Sammie. During the course of the conversation, they discussed their ages. He told her that he was 32 and soon to be 33, what? She did not believe him and told him so. When he learned that she was just 16 he told her that he did not believe her and that caused some laughter from both of them. It felt good to freely laugh since she had not done so in quite some time and he had easily gotten her to laugh. As the conversation progressed, she learned he was divorced with four kids; his ex-wife had his daughter and youngest son; he had his oldest and middle sons. She should have told him right then and there that she was not interested, but something kept her from doing that. Suzie was intrigued. They made plans to go out the following day after she finished work, but she told him that he would have to come over to meet Jim and Carol. "Not a problem," he said. A fit of laughter engulfed her as she imagined a 32 year old man meeting parents. Incredible. He was easily making her laugh and that was something she had not done in a while.

Chapter 4

Following a mostly sleepless night, dawn crept into her room where she had cried so much from the memory of the rape and she was not feeling good about anything that morning. She was convinced that someone like Sammie would not be interested if he ever found out and it just did not seem fair that she would never be able to have normalcy because of what others had done to her. Maybe she should just end this before anything got started, she could tell him that he was too old which would be easy because he honestly was. Her brain was telling her that was the right thing to do, but her heart was stuck on an emphatic no, plus she wasn't sure what her parents would say. There was a huge possibility that they would not allow her to see him if they had any idea how old he was, she was only 16 after all. What a night, not much sleep and she was going to see this Adonis again. Thank God Jean had taught her how to do stage makeup, a skill she would utilize so no one would know that she had very little sleep.

Sundays were usually pretty slow and this one was slower than normal, two o'clock could not come soon enough. Suzie wanted time to get home so she could shower, clean up and make herself up to hide the sleeplessness. Finally, the day ended, but the drive home seemed to take forever. There were few traffic lights in Martin's Cove but it seemed every one of them was red which caused unwanted delays. Jim and Carol knew that this new guy was coming over that afternoon and Jim teased Suzie about bringing the shotgun out which made her smile. Dressed and ready, Sammie arrived right on time, points for that.

Jim and Carol were gracious, as was Sammie. Suzie calmed down a bit when it was obvious that Sammie's charm had won Carol over. She could not stop looking at him and smiling. Jim started asking some pretty intense questions. Suzie was aware of some of Sammie's history and it made her nervous that Jim would figure out how old he was.

Sammie was raised in Brookwood, a town located next to Petersville where he served on the volunteer fire department prior to his time in the Army and Jim had

23

been a volunteer fireman in Petersville. Sammie's parents owned an ice company not far from where Jim and Carol's house was in Petersville and since Jim was contracted by that town to plow snow in the winter, Suzie calculated pretty quickly that her father was going to figure this out. By the expression on her father's face, she knew right then and there that he was familiar with Sammie's parents and probably knew he was a lot older than his daughter. Sammie did not hide any detail except that he was divorced and had children for which Suzie was grateful.

Apparently, Jim was okay with this and let Suzie go with Sammie which was a bit perplexing. Suzie would learn years later that her father allowed her to see him because he knew how devastated she had been when they left Petersville and never felt like she fit in at Martin's Cove. He also knew that something serious had happened to her and thought if he allowed her the freedom to see Sammie then it might help her get back to what she used to be. Jim trusted her.

Sammie opened the car door for Suzie and helped her in as he told her she looked sensational. Impressive manners. They drove up the hill and stopped, looked at each other and laughed at the way her parents had reacted. Due to the fact that Suzie was well under age, they went to the local A&W so they could get something to eat and talk privately in the car. Suzie asked Sammie why he had told her father so much information and he told her that if they were going to get to know one another, he did not want any lies told. We tell the truth and figure it out from there which makes sense.

Sammie told her about his ex-wife and his other two children, Cara and Jack whom he missed tremendously and did not like it that his children would not grow up together. He then told her about Sam and Teddy, the two boys who lived with him. They sounded like good kids, but Suzie was apprehensive about meeting them so soon. What would they think? Were they used to him bringing women home? She asked him and he told her no, but he just felt it was right to introduce her to them. What did she know, she didn't have any kids and since he was their father she figured he knew what he was doing.

They drove to Sammie's house. She was nervous, after all, she had just spent a little while with Sammie alone and now she was going to meet his kids. Sammie came around to open the door for her and she slid out of his car. He surprised her by scooping her up in his arms and carrying her up the stairs, which was a bit embarrassing since the boys were upstairs. She did not see them immediately and that made her feel a bit better as he called them into the living room so introductions could be made. Suzie instantly liked them. Sam was the older of the two and had this suspicious look on his face, one that Suzie would later refer to as his 'mad' look, Teddy was more engaging and talkative. Suzie attributed this to their ages. Sammie had brought food for them and he told them to go in their rooms to eat and they did. He walked over to the stereo asking what kind of music she liked and she told him that she enjoyed the music of the 1950's and 1960's. Smiling, he chose some of the oldies which tend to be on the romantic side and what he choose to play certainly hit the mark.

Sammie walked over to the sofa where Suzie sat, held out his hand which she took and he gently pulled her into his arms to dance. What? Where are the cameras she thought, this stuff only happens in the movies. He was a very good dancer and they danced for a couple of songs when he suddenly stopped. He looked down at her and told her that she was the most beautiful girl he had ever seen which caused her to blush. He gently placed a hand on either side of her face and slowly went to kiss her. In that second, every moment of the rape played through her mind and she slapped him. She broke from his grasp and retreated to the sofa. God, what had she just done, this was going to end before it even began.

Sammie stood stunned for a moment then went to the sofa but sat on the coffee table facing her. She had her face in her hands and he pulled her hands away asking what he had done and what was wrong. She could not speak nor was she sure that she wanted to tell him as tears ran down her face and her only thought was her mother's word – 'whore'. Sammie was gentle but persistent, reminding her that if they were going to get to know one another she could not hide anything from him, honesty was important. She slowly looked up at him, took a deep breath and choked out the words, "I was raped." She hung her head expecting a negative reaction. He was speechless and started to put his arms around her but pulled back, thinking better of that at the moment. He quietly asked her what happened, where and when; without looking up, she told him the story. His first reaction was to get angry, pacing the living room wanting to seek justice for her, then he went to her and without thinking he pulled her into his arms. Reluctantly, she let him hold her, they stayed that way for what seemed like an eternity and he didn't seem to mind that her tears were soaking his shirt. She asked, "With what happened and our age difference what do you want with me?" Holding her tight he said, "You are an amazingly beautiful woman, smart, funny, and I knew the moment I saw you in the store that I wanted to get to know you. You intrigue me." Could she trust what he was saying? She just let him hold her because for the first time in a very long time, she began to feel safe and protected.

"Only You" by the Platters started playing. Sammie slid his hand up to her chin, tilted her head and very gently touched his lips to hers. Even though she couldn't bring herself to respond, the fireworks exploding in that room seemed endless as did their kiss. He was gentle yet commanding. Could this be possible after enduring such a horrific event? "Oh, Suzie, you are amazing. I want to know every bit of you and I vow to you right here and now that we will make this work," he told her. This was a little too much to take in but Suzie decided that she wanted to get to know him also. One can't explain feelings and what she was feeling amazed her even with the apprehension that clouded the moment.

Music, as with most couples, would become very important to them over the course of time and "Only You" was the first of many songs that would be added to their play list. Many other things would become important also, including the two young faces that were peeking around the corner. Suzie smiled when she saw them. They scampered away and she wondered if they had ever seen their parents like this because she had never seen her parents like this. She smiled as Sammie's lips found

26

hers again, his kisses were so gentle, caring, and she wondered if she could trust that this was real after what had happened to her.

Intense conversation took place as to what they were doing and how they would manage to see each other, then it was time to leave. Sammie gingerly lifted her into his arms and carried her to the car, a habit she would come to enjoy. On the ride home she was a bit nervous because she did not know what her father was going to say. Would he put a stop to them seeing each other? She really hoped not. They arrived at her house and he opened the car door for her. Walking her to the door, he was careful to stay behind her and she noticed his manners. At the door she knew there would be no kiss, her father was watching and they both knew that. Sammie took her hand, brought it to his lips and told her that he would call her the next day. As she watched him leave, she thought that it must be time to wake up because this had to be a dream.

She had anticipated a barrage of questions, but none came. Her father just simply asked if she had a good time. Of course she had and she said so. She went to her parents' room, called Kim who had started dating an older guy and Suzie wanted to know what she thought of their vast age difference. Kim told her to just go with the flow and see what happens, she could hear the excitement in Suzie's voice. Of course, the maturity level of the older guys far exceeded any of the boys at school and this was refreshing because Suzie felt that guys their age were jerks. Most were at 16 or 17.

While lying in bed that night, thoughts of the afternoon replayed through her mind and she could still feel the touch of his lips on hers. Oh, brother, she was more intrigued by him than before and this proved a bit unsettling. The age difference crept into her thoughts and she knew it would rear its ugly head at some point which scared her. She decided that even after her revelation and his reaction she was going to give it time to see how things went. After all, he had at least done all the right things today. Somewhere around four in the morning she drifted off to sleep with the words to "Only You" echoing through her head.

Chapter 5

Summer school went quickly that day, Suzie still had a couple of hours to kill before she had to be at work so she went home to get something to eat. While there, Sammie called her and asked if she could stop by his house on the way home from work. She told her mother she was going to Kim's after work, Carol said fine and reminded her to be home by eleven. Fine, and out the door she went.

Work was busy and even if it were slow, she would find a way to keep busy because busy days meant quicker days and that is what she wanted today, a quick afternoon. She felt the butterflies of anticipation in her stomach as she left work that evening. There had to be a discussion about the age difference and how they were going to manage to spend time together because she was concerned about her father. She also wanted to know something else, what he wanted with her, she was damaged and so young. With so much on her mind, pulling into the driveway left her feeling uneasy but quickly the uneasiness turned to ecstasy when she saw him standing there waiting for her. Helping her out of the car and scooping her into his arms, they started up the stairs. She still felt a little uneasy about this, wondering if it would last.

The boys came out of their rooms and they talked a bit together before they disappeared out the door. Sammie went to the stereo and turned on the music, walked to the sofa with his hand extended, he pulled Suzie to him and danced her around the living room. He could sense the apprehension and tension in her body and asked what was wrong.

Suzie: "We really need to talk a bit."

Sammie: "Sure."

Suzie sat on the sofa and Sammie on the coffee table, a table he would come to hate with time.

Sammie: "What's wrong?"

Suzie: "How are we going to deal with our age difference and what do you find so fascinating about me? I'm a kid and not much older than Sam."

Sammie: "Suzie, you are beautiful, funny, and smart and I really want to get to know you. How do you feel about being with someone my age? Does it really bother you?"

Suzie: "I'm not sure how I feel, I'm really confused. It bothers me that my father isn't going to like it if I see you a lot. We aren't going to be able to go out publicly because so many people know my father and me for that matter, and I just don't get it. How are we going to deal with that and how am I going to get here as much as you are going to want me to be here and as much as I'm going to want to be here?"

Sammie: "We will deal with the situation as it is for now, we will spend as much time together as we possibly can and if your father tries to stop us, we will figure something out. How is your mother with this? We can go out publicly if we leave town and we will do that. I don't get it either, but we can't always explain what we feel."

Suzie: "My mother could care less. All she does is call me a whore because of the clothes I wear but she hasn't said anything about you at all. I do know she likes you but I'm not worried about her, I'm more worried about my father. I think he figured out how old you are by the things you two discussed yesterday."

Sammie: "Let's take this one day at a time and we will figure it out. I really do like you and what happened to you doesn't matter to me. It wasn't your fault, you didn't ask them to rape you and as time goes on, I will help you get through it. I promise. Your age doesn't matter to me, it's just a number."

Sammie moved to sit next to Suzie on the sofa and put his arm around her. He started talking about his boys. Of course this was new to the kids so he wasn't sure how they felt yet about having Suzie around. He shared that their mother was supposed to switch the kids for the summer that that hadn't happened that year and he didn't like it. He missed Cara and Jack a lot and wished they were close enough to see them more often. His sadness was evident. The boys were going to be home most of the summer alone except when he took them to his mother's house when they would be gone for at least a week, maybe two.

Suzie: "When are they going to your mom's?"

30

Sammie: "It will be in a couple of weeks."

Suzie: "That will be a good break for them and you too."

Sammie: "When the boys are at my moms would you like to spend the weekend with me? Can you manage to do that? That is if you want to?"

Suzie: I guess I can switch my work schedule around and tell my parents I'm at Kim's, she'll cover for me."

Sammie: "I hate that you will have to lie. I didn't want any part of our relationship based on lies."

Suzie: "I know, I don't like it either but it's the only thing I can think to do. Sammie, what if I'm not ready to spend the night with you? I know what that's going to mean and I'm not sure I'm ready."

Sammie: "If you aren't ready, then we'll wait. I'm not going to push you into anything. I want you to want this as much as I do. If you think you may want to stay with me, I need to ask if you are doing anything about birth control. I hate to bring that up right now, but I have four kids and I really don't want any more, especially right now."

Suzie: "Yes, after I was raped I went to the doctor a couple weeks later and went on the pill. I don't want to get pregnant, especially that way. Besides, I'm too young for that and I'm not even sure I want kids. I don't know what I would have done if I had gotten pregnant."

Sammie: "You know, I am really looking forward to our future. I know it's soon and early but I do like you a lot. I know it's soon for you, but I want you to feel the same way someday."

Suzie: "Neither one of us knows what the future will hold for us, let's take this one day at a time. I don't know when I'm going to be able to come back again because my work schedule is for the next couple of nights. Besides if I'm gone all the time, my father might start giving me a hard time."

With that, Sammie got up and pulled Suzie into his arms which felt strong, secure and safe. Suzie was still a bit hesitant but was beginning to like the way she felt when she was with him. He took his hand and lifted her chin, bringing his lips to hers, nothing ever felt as good as that kiss did at that moment. His lips were warm, soft and all consuming. Suzie felt herself starting to relax and respond, it just seemed

31

natural and she knew in that moment that she was going to have to try hard to trust him even though that was going to be a challenge for her. After being raped, trust was not something that would come easily.

They heard the boys returning and they were laughing, it was such a sweet sound. Suzie spent a lot of time babysitting for kids the last few years and enjoyed kids. She also had her own brother, Joe, who was the same age as Sam and she wondered if they knew each other from school, but she didn't want to ask.

Attempting to lighten the mood the discussion changed to different things they each liked, and they learned they did not share too many interests. Their taste in music was the same, they both hated television, they basically liked the same kinds of food and both of them liked being outside, just enough to make them want to pursue a relationship. Sammie ran his hands down her arms and told her that he was glad that she was beginning to relax a little with him, he would strive to have her become more and more comfortable with him.

What was this man doing to her? The thought haunted her as she prepared to leave, this was a new concept for her and she was becoming more intrigued. Walking down the stairs was not an option as she found herself securely in his arms. Setting Suzie down, Sammie saw her look up to the sky. The stars were brilliant, so many, and so busy.

Sammie: "Close your eyes and make a wish."

Complying, her wish came from her heart.

Sammie: "Shh, you see the big dipper over there? I want to fill that dipper with wishes and dreams for us to share."

Suzie: "That is so sweet. Did you make a wish?"

Sammie: "Of course, but I can't tell you because then it won't come true."

Suzie smiled and their lips met. As she drove home, her confusion was battling a war with the things Sammie had told her. She knew in her heart that she really wanted to see where this was going to go, admitting to herself that she really did like him, but, was it right? He is 32, she 16, what were they doing? Wishing those negative voices would stop, she decided as she pulled in the driveway that she was going to make an effort to just let this happen and see where it went. Sometimes, she hated that she tried to analyze everything.

Arriving home was not pleasant, Carol and Jim must have had an argument because Carol was stomping around the house and Jim sat in his chair pretending to watch something on the television. The tension was thick and quite evident as soon as she walked in the house. Since this was occurring regularly Suzie wondered what they were even doing together, she could never imagine things being this way with Sammie. She went to her room with intentions of getting some much needed sleep. She put some records on the record player and around two in the morning she fell asleep listening to the songs Sammie had played for her, and thoughts of how his lips felt on hers.

Chapter 6

During the next several days Suzie was busy with summer school and work which was good because they would not be able to see each other too much. It was a time of some very deep thoughts and intense conversations with Kim. Kim was obviously excited that Suzie had found someone who seemed so nice. Suzie told Kim that she was having a lot of anxiety over the fact that Sammie wanted her to spend the weekend with him. How would she know what to do because she knew what his intentions were? Kim assured her that since he was older, he would know how to guide her through everything. They arranged for Suzie to say that she would be spending that weekend with Kim and Kim's mother was okay with that also. Oh how she wished her parents were like Kim's who accepted the fact that Kim was with Gary even though he was much older than her. They also talked of getting together soon so they could all meet Sammie.

After work for the next several nights, Sammie called her right about the time she walked in the door inquiring about her day, talking for a while then serenading her with "Goodnight Sweetheart." This guy was incredibly romantic and certainly knew how to make things seem so right. After they talked the third night, Suzie's father called her into the living room stating he was concerned that she was spending a bit too much time concentrated on Sammie. Suzie assured him that this was not the case, she had school, work and plans which seemed to appease him for the moment.

Saturday was approaching and the work schedule was to work the morning shift so they would finally be able to see each other again after almost a week. As always, Suzie told her parents she was going to Kim's after work. Carol told her to be home by ten and Jim told her midnight was good. This is how it had always been, one saying one thing and the other saying something else. Jim would run interference with Carol but it was always a fight and of course Suzie being Suzie, she would listen to Jim.

Work was good. Jean was working that Saturday and it was always fun when she was there. She had been teaching her make-up skills to Suzie and they had two make-overs scheduled for that morning and Suzie liked doing them. Jean had taught her how to use the make-up to turn some pretty rough looking women into beauties and this day, Jean would have one and Suzie the other. Suzie had quite a collection of her own make-up and was skilled at making herself up also. The day went very quickly and before she knew it, it was time to go.

When she arrived at Sammie's house, she was met in the driveway. How did he know when she would get there, she wondered. It was so good to see him, he was so handsome and his smile was winning. Of course, she did not have to walk up the stairs. She joked with him about him getting a hernia and their laughter filled the living room. It was quiet and she wondered where they boys were. Sammie told her they were with friends and they would have a few hours alone which was the first time they would be truly alone for more than an hour or so. "In the Still of the Night" was playing on the stereo, he took her in his arms and danced her around the living room. He was an amazing dancer, and she liked that.

When the music stopped he slid his hands to her face, looked into her eyes and told her just how beautiful she was then slowly brought his lips to hers. That kiss was amazing, his lips were soft yet firm and the passion was enough to heat up the already warm room to the point of taking her breath away. For the first time since that wonderful day when they met, she kissed him back and could immediately feel his response. That made her a little nervous and she pulled away. Without words he figured out what had happened and went to the kitchen to get them something to drink because he had to do something to hide his desire for her, he did not want to scare her.

During their conversation they shared laughter and that felt good, he was making it easy for her to do so. The conversation covered multiple subjects, was easy, and his voice was smooth as silk. Suzie went to light a cigarette, a habit that he did not like at all, he leaned over and kissed her hard telling her that every time she went to light a cigarette, he was going to kiss her so she would stop that filthy habit. She vowed to herself that she would have to work on quitting.

Sammie: "Are you going to be able to spend the weekend with me when I take the kids to my mom's?"

Suzie: "I spoke with Kim and she is going to cover me for Friday and Saturday nights. Her mother is okay with it also. The plans are shopping Saturday, out that night and Sunday there is going to be a cook out and I'll stay for that. I'll have to be home by about eight o'clock Sunday night. Is that good?"

Sammie: "That is perfect. I will take Friday off so I can take the boys to Mom's and they will be gone for the next week, maybe two."

He moved to the coffee table. She knew that the conversation was going to turn serious and apprehension settled in her stomach.

Sammie: "Suzie, that weekend is going to be very special. I would love to take you to the bedroom right now but I want this to be perfect for you, for us and I don't want to rush you."

Suzie: "You told me in the beginning that if this was going to work I had to be honest with you in all things. Well, I am really nervous. You know what happened to me and I don't want that to ruin our special time. I'm so afraid it will."

Sammie: "I will be very gentle with you. I want you to remember 'us' and not how it was for you then. That's not what making love is all about, it is tender, caring and can be very beautiful. I know being with you is going to be amazing and I'll guide you. If I start to do anything you aren't comfortable with you just tell me to 'stop' and I will, I promise."

Suzie: "I am going to trust you and you know that's really hard for me to do. I just don't want to be hurt again."

Pulling her into his arms,

Sammie: "I would never hurt you. This is going to be better than you could ever imagine."

Suzie: "Well, since you were married you are used to having sex, I'm not so I guess I have to believe you."

Sammie: "With each person it is different. Most of it will depend on your feelings for me as it will depend on my feelings for you. I'm telling you this now, I have extremely strong feelings for you already and I promise to make this very special for you. Something you will never forget for the rest of your life."

They held each other for a long time without saying a word, they didn't have to. The boys would not be back for about an hour and Sammie suggested they go out to get something to eat. Since they did not have much time something quick would have to do and A&W was quick. Instead of eating there, they brought the food home and of course brought something for the boys. The boys came in and they sat around the coffee table to eat which was a treat for them, they liked A&W and eating in the living room made it special. The conversation was about what the boys were going to do for the summer, it was evident that they were excited to be going to their grandmother's house.

It was a carefree afternoon and evening, the boys actually talked more than previously and it all seemed so natural. Suzie noticed that Sam talked more than he had previously but still had that mad look about him. Thinking of her brother who was the same age she attributed it to his age, too old to be a kid but too young to be old enough. Teddy was different, he was more talkative, sometimes too much so but it was never squashed, at least not with Suzie. They were really good boys and Suzie liked them.

After they went to their rooms, Sammie and Suzie talked of when they could see each other again and how often the next week. It was going to be difficult because of her work schedule and the fact that she didn't want her father figuring out that they were seeing each other a lot. She also mentioned that she was concerned what the boys would think if she was around all the time. She had already made plans with Kim for the next Saturday to go shopping so they would just have a few hours that evening and she could stop by after work that Sunday. Plans were set and the rest of their short time together was spent cuddled together on the sofa quietly talking about nothing and everything, striving to learn more about each other.

Time was the enemy, Suzie had to leave. For the first time, she honestly did not want to leave. Oh my, what was happening here? Could this work? Only time will tell. As Sammie gathered her in his arms for the journey down the stairs, she encircled his neck with her arms eliciting a smile. The stars were brilliant and again, they made a wish. Setting her gently down, he took her in his arms and brought his lips to hers, giving her a gentle, loving kiss to end a perfectly wonderful day. While looking deeply into her eyes, he started singing, "Goodnight Sweetheart." The drive home was a little sad, she did not want to leave him. She liked the way she felt when she was with him and did not want it to end. She was hooked and had no doubt that he was also.

Friday was a day off from everything so Kim and Suzie planned on shopping, Suzie needed something special to wear the following weekend. The plan was that Suzie would be spending the weekend with Kim and since that was not unusual it would cover her for her weekend with Sammie. Kim's mom was okay with covering for Suzie so it made it a bit easier even though she did not like lying. In case something came up, Suzie gave Kim Sammie's phone number.

While shopping, Suzie shared her apprehension about the next weekend with Kim and she assured her that since Sammie was older he would be able to guide her as he had said and you can always tell him to stop if he does something you aren't comfortable with. That sounded easy, but Kim was not aware of what had happened to Suzie the previous year. Setting all her mixed up feelings aside, shopping was fun and Suzie found a fabulous outfit for her weekend, but wondered if she should purchase a special nightgown. Kim laughed and told her not to worry about that because it wouldn't be on that long anyway and they both shared a good laugh.

Since Suzie was off Saturday, she stopped at Sammie's on the way home from shopping. Of course, he was waiting for her in the driveway. She never saw her father treat her mother this way and wondered if this was just to impress her. After gently kissing her, he carried her up the stairs to an eerily quiet house. Sammie had taken the boys to his mother's house the previous day and it just didn't seem normal.

Suzie suddenly had a case of nerves and Sammie picked up on it immediately. He did not put any pressure on her at all, he was always very kind and gentle with her. What was all this, she wondered, was this normal?

> Sammie: "What's bothering you?"
>
> Suzie: "How did you know that something was bothering me?" I was just wondering why you always carry me up and down the stairs when I come and go. And, I am nervous."
>
> Sammie: "I can tell when something is bothering you. I'm just showing you how much I care for you. Don't you like it? And being nervous is totally expected, we will be fine."
>
> Suzie: "Hasn't this all happened a bit quickly and yes, of course I like it."
>
> Sammie" "Suzie, I really care for you. I have since the first time I laid eyes on you. I want you to know how I feel about you."
>
> Suzie: "I was just curious because I've never seen my father treat my mother the way you treat me."
>
> Sammie: "I'm not your father and because I care about you so much, I want to show it, not just say it. I want you to always be sure of how I feel about you."
>
> Suzie: "Okay, I was just curious. I like you a lot too and I'm working on trusting you. You are making that easier than I thought it would be and I'm trying to get used to all of the new feelings I am feeling."
>
> Sammie: "I hope you do get used to everything because I don't plan on treating you any differently and as time goes on, it will only get better."

They talked more, mostly about the next weekend's plans. He just smiled at her but thought about her lying and did not like it. He knew that she did not like it either but at this time, it couldn't be helped.

> Sammie: "I want next weekend to be so special for you, for us. I know I've said that before but I mean it. I really feel like this is going to be the beginning of our lives together."
>
> Suzie: "The beginning of our lives together started when you walked into the store that afternoon, but I know what you mean.

40

I'm just nervous and I want the weekend to be special for you too and I'm just not sure I know how to do that."

Gathering her in his arms, he whispered, "Every second I spend with you has been and is going to continue to be special. As long as I know you are enjoying yourself then it will be special for me."

Suzie smiled when he kissed her. It seemed that every time they were together it was getting more and more comfortable. She was right where she wanted to be. With all of his kisses and Suzie thinking about the next weekend, she started giggling causing Sammie to look at her inquisitively. Never having been with anyone seriously, she wasn't sure what that nervous, tickly feeling was. She shared this with him and he smiled broadly. He told her that was only a normal feeling of desire. She blushed as she smiled and decided she was liking this even though her age reared its ugly head at the wrong times sometimes.

They sat on the sofa talking for the rest of their time together. She learned more about the other two kids and he reiterated how much he missed them. They talked of the boys and how excited they were to be at his mother's, how much she enjoyed having them but could only take them for short periods of time. Suzie learned that the boys liked her which she thought was sweet and told him that she really liked them also. Then he told her that his mother wanted to meet her. What? She had not expected that so soon, she asked him when he was picking the boys up. He told her that they would be there for the next two weeks, but she had to work and could not ask for another weekend off for a bit because of taking the next weekend off. Meeting his mother would have to wait and Suzie was relieved.

It was time to leave, even though she would rather stay where she was than go home, but there had not been any issues and this would just have to be the way it was going to be for a while. They both knew it was going to be difficult for the next year and a half until she turned 18 and then no one could say a thing. He carried her down the stairs where they paused in the driveway and looked up at the sky. They made their wishes to put in the Big Dipper. Her wish that night was that time would go quickly so she would never have to leave.

Driving home was just going to be too quick so Suzie detoured down to the lake, the back side. Since she was raped, she did not go to the main beach any longer and would never go again, because the memories were just too difficult to deal with. The back side offered her solace. She was still having some reservations about their planned weekend, wondering if what they were going to do was right. Then she started thinking about how she felt when she was with him. Is this how everyone felt when they were with someone they really cared about? If it was, she was going to have to get used to these feelings because she was beginning to like them.

When she drove into the driveway, she saw that her father was in the garage. He was obviously angry because he was throwing his tools on the workbench which meant they were fighting again. She went into the garage with her shopping bags and asked her father if something had broken, he just groaned. She went upstairs to find her mother in the kitchen and it was obvious that she had been crying. Why couldn't she just have a happy family? Instead of asking to see what Suzie had purchased, her mother just made a comment about her finding more whore clothes. Suzie just went to her room. Even though her mother tried to make her feel like a whore she knew that she was not one. She wished her mother trusted her and wanted to enjoy spending time with her as Kim's mom did with Kim. Putting all that aside, all Suzie wanted to think about was the coming weekend. She wanted that weekend to be as special as Sammie told her it would be especially after coming home to all this tension, this was going to be a long week. She added to her diary, filling the pages with everything about Sammie.

Chapter 7

As predicted, the week seemed to drag on and it was almost unbearable. The schedule at work each day was from three in the afternoon until closing. She had Friday off which would be another long day since Sammie did not get out of work until five in the afternoon. She wondered what she would do with the whole day to herself because she did not want to stay home. She decided that shopping for part of the afternoon would help make the day go faster and she had not been to the local mall in a while.

Friday finally arrived, Suzie took great care getting dressed in her new outfit, a simple summer dress and sandals. Gazing at herself in the mirror she wondered what Sammie would think, she hoped he would like it. She packed her bag with a couple of other outfits just as cute as the one she had on, her make-up and she was ready. She left the house at one in the afternoon leaving time to get some lunch and look around the mall. Suddenly her nerves got the best of her and she double checked to make sure she had her birth control pills thinking how good it was that she worked in a pharmacy, she was able to acquire such things without her parents knowing.

When she got in the car, she noticed something sticking out from under the visor. It was a note from her father.

> Slip, I know what you are doing this weekend. Don't let him hurt you. I don't like you seeing him, he's too old for you but I also know you. Have fun and make sure it's special. Love, Dad.

Oh my God, how did he know? Her father had always had a special connection with her but this was beyond anything he had ever done and it served to unnerve her. She went to the A&W. Sitting quietly in the car while she ate something gave her time to think about what her father had written. Was she doing the right thing? Was Sammie really too old for her? She knew in the deep recesses of her mind that he was and all the doubts that she had previously resurfaced. Since she did her best thinking while driving, she decided to go for a ride, shopping was not necessary. She had about four hours before Sammie would be home so she just drove with no destination in mind.

For the next couple of hours she ran the pros and cons of Sammie through her head. Yes, he was older, had kids and was divorced, however, there had never been anyone else in her life who treated her the way he did, made all the bad things seem okay, and he certainly acted like he cherished her. She was beginning to feel comfortable with him and realized that she was also beginning to trust him. With that in mind, she turned the car around and headed towards her fate.

When she arrived, Sammie's car was not in the garage but alongside of the driveway with the garage door open. He appeared in the driveway and motioned for her to pull into the garage. He had already showered and was dressed rather nicely in gray slacks and a blue shirt. She looked at him and thought how very handsome he was. She never would have thought that she would get so lucky to have met someone like him. All her nervousness disappeared and she knew more than ever that she was doing the right thing. He opened the door for her and she got out of the car thinking he not only looked great but he smelled good which caused her nerves to flair.

Sammie: "Suzie, you look absolutely amazing. That outfit looks really good on you but more importantly you make that outfit look good."

Suzie: "Sammie, you look wonderful too, and smell so good. I'm nervous."

Sammie: "I knew you would be and it's okay. I'd rather have you nervous than over confident."

Suzie: "Well confident certainly is one thing I am not."

He closed the garage door and slipped her into his arms for a kiss that seemed to ignite all the fireworks available for Fourth of July. He managed to have this effect on her and she wondered if she had the same effect on him when suddenly she realized that she did. He took her bag and gently lifted her into his arms for the trip upstairs. She could hear "Heaven on Earth" by the Platters playing on the stereo.

44

He set her down gently at the top of the stairs, went around the corner with her bag and suddenly she felt self-conscious. When he walked into the living room he immediately sensed her nervousness and went right to her, held her at arm-length, looked her up and down, told her again that she looked absolutely beautiful. He took her hand and guided her to the sofa, setting her down. He sat on the coffee table, the damn table, meant serious stuff and Suzie did not want to hear anything serious right now. He took her hands and gently squeezed them.

> Sammie: "Suzie, tonight is going to be the first of hopefully many nights together. I always want you to remember these moments. This is not only the first time for us to be together, but it is the first time for you. What happened to you before was just sex, it was crude, cold and without feeling. This is going to be so different. We are going to make love, it's going to be warm, tender, and loving."
>
> Suzie: "How do you always know what I'm feeling?"
>
> Sammie: "I care about you more than you think I do and more than I thought, that makes me sensitive to you and your needs. In time, you will learn to respond to my moods."
>
> Suzie: "I guess that will happen. I don't know, I've never been with anyone seriously before."
>
> Sammie: "I know and we are going to make some wonderful memories and someday it will be just you and me. Before we do anything, I started dinner for us. I'm going to go finish it and you can change the music if you'd like."
>
> Suzie: "Ok, do you want to hear anything in particular?"
>
> Sammie: "Whatever you like."

When she went to the stereo she noticed that the dining room table was set, graced with lit candles and the china from the china cabinet. She wondered what he had cooked, it didn't smell too bad. She knew he fed the boys but she wasn't sure how good he was in the kitchen, this would be interesting. Going through his records, she noticed he only had one Elvis album which would have to change since she liked Elvis. She chose that, two by the Platters and another by The Five Satins, all of which were good mood music. While fixing the stereo, she heard pots banging, what sounded like a spoon hitting the floor and a resounding "Oh shit" from the kitchen. She started laughing but was told to stay in the living room so she stood by the stereo looking out of the living room window. Her thoughts went back to the note she found in the car but decided not to tell him about it.

Totally engrossed in her thoughts, she did not hear him come up behind her. She jumped when he touched her. He had caught her off guard and she laughed although her heart was pounding. She turned to him, he enfolded her in his arms and kissed her very tenderly. Then he led her to the table where he had set out the spaghetti dinner he had prepared. Well that wasn't too terribly difficult and she was sure that he prepared it for the boys so it was something he surely knew how to do. It didn't smell too bad, there was Italian bread, butter and soda filled her glass. Wine would have been good but she was under age and he never offered her anything alcoholic nor had she ever seen him drink. Good, he didn't have a drinking problem or so she thought.

He put some spaghetti on her plate, making her nervous that he was watching her so intently. She took a bit of the food and tried very hard not to choke, it was awful. She did manage to tell him it was good so he would stop staring at her. Suzie was Italian and had grown up with homemade pasta sauce, this was obviously doctored up from a jar. How could she eat this without letting him know it was horrible? The bread would work. They ate in relative silence and she had to work hard at letting him think it was good. Some day she would have to help him improve his culinary skills.

When they finished eating, he started to clear the table, Suzie rose to help him take some dishes into the kitchen where she almost dropped them. She started laughing, she couldn't help it, the kitchen was a holy mess. There was sauce all over the stove, pots in the sink, what the heck had he done? She wanted to help clean up and he said no that he would do it later. He went to the refrigerator to get two plates, each containing a piece of pie and a can of whipped cream that he set on the counter. He told her to put some whipped cream on the pies. As she started for the can, he suddenly grabbed her, held her close to him, took the whipped cream and squirted some in her mouth. He was laughing as he squirted some in his mouth. She was trying to swallow between laughing and the whipped cream that started to drip out of her mouth. He leaned down and kissed her with both of their mouths filled with whipped cream. She felt his tongue slip into her mouth and she let him. Their tongues danced together and he tickled the roof of her mouth with his tongue. This was her first French kiss and she rather liked it. Not only were fireworks going off in that kitchen, but so was every other fire device known to man.

He started dancing her around the kitchen, slowly making his way into the living room with her in his arms. When he tried to set her down on the sofa she mentioned that she had to use the rest room, the pie all but forgotten. While she was gone, he had retrieved the gift from the bedroom and placed it on the coffee table. When she returned, she inquired about what it was and with a sheepish grin he said, "a gift." She sat down, slowly opened the gift, and the contents took her breath away. Inside of the box was the most gorgeous negligee she had ever seen in her life, not that she had seen many but it was beautiful. It was long, the lightest of blue, had an empire waist with spaghetti straps that dropped down the plunging back and a lacy bodice. There was also a matching robe and slippers. It was stunning and brought tears to her eyes as Sammie simply smiled. Her nerves started flaring as she thought, oh my, he wants me to wear this for him? He simply continued to smile and gestured for her to go into the bathroom to change.

Suzie took the box with her to go and change. She did so slowly, wondering what she was going to do since she had never been exposed to anything like this previously and she wanted this to be special for him as it obviously was going to be for her. She looked at herself in the mirror and had to admit, he had picked the perfect size and she did look rather stunning. She put on the robe, tied the sash, and slipped on the slippers that were the same blue with a small heel and a band of feathers. This was amazing and she felt like a million dollars. She made sure that her hair was perfect, took a very deep breath and with butterflies soaring in her stomach she slowly opened the door to greet her fate.

While she had been changing, Sammie had scattered rose petals all over the floor, the bedroom door was closed so she could not see in there but she noticed reflecting flickering light on the wall and knew he had lit candles. Of course there was music playing, soft and very romantic. Slowly she stepped from the hallway to the living room when Sammie looked up and just stared at her, slowly letting his lips curl into a smile that shot straight to her heart. It was obvious he wanted to say something but could not get the words out when Suzie noticed a single tear roll down his cheek and the look on his face. Oh my, to have this kind of effect on someone was pretty special she thought. Finally he managed to say, "Suzie, you are stunningly beautiful."

Suzie stood there, not exactly knowing what to do next when Sammie rose, went to her, took her by the hand and encouraged her further into the living room. He turned her around slowly and seemed more in awe than when he had first laid eyes on her. Standing before her, he reached down to undo the belt to the robe. He then moved his hands to her shoulders and pushed the robe aside, letting it float to the floor. He just stood there looking at her, turning her slowly around to see that plunging back and again, she noticed the single tear roll down his cheek. The look on his face spoke louder than any words he could say. It was obvious how he felt.

Sammie: "I have never seen anyone as beautiful as you are right now.

Suzie you are so special, so absolutely beautiful and I am very lucky to have you here with me right now."

Suzie smiled at him as he took her into his arms and kissed her with a passion that she had yet experienced. Desire exploded within her as she felt the strength of his hands against her exposed back. This must be what she had read about in books because every inch of her tingled. At that moment, she wasn't sure what to do but she knew that she wanted him more than anything else in the world.

He had a way of making her feel so safe after what had happened to her and that alone calmed her nerves. She let the memory of that instant in time burn itself into her heart.

Chapter 8

Gathering her up in his arms, he carried her toward the bedroom without ever taking his eyes off of hers. When he opened the bedroom door, she could see the candles flickering and the bed was covered with red and white rose pedals. There were flowers on either side of the bed and pillows scattered on the bed under the rose petals. He gently set her down in the middle of the bed, reached down and slowly removed each of the slippers dropping them to the floor keeping his eyes fixed on hers. He sat on the bed next to her, took her face in his hands and kissed her lips, letting their tongues play together. Finally breaking the kiss, he looked at her and smiled, Suzie was beyond nervous.

> Sammie: "Suzie I know you are all kinds of nervous so we are going to take this very slowly. I don't want to touch you because I don't want to do anything that will scare you. I want you to touch me wherever you like, then I will touch you in the same place. This way you are guiding me. We can go as slow as you like, we have all night."
>
> Suzie: "Ok, I guess. I am really nervous and I want you to enjoy yourself also."
>
> Sammie: "I will enjoy anything we do as long as I know you are happy."

Sammie smiled as Suzie placed her hands on either side of his face, her hands were soft and her touch was gentle. She started to caress his cheeks, using her thumbs to tease his lips as he followed her lead and did the same to her. She wanted to know what it would be like for him to touch her all over but did not want to seem over anxious. Slowly she drew her hands down his neck to his shoulders.

> Suzie: "This isn't fair, you have too many clothes on."
>
> Sammie: "You can take some of them off if you'd like."

Taking a deep breath, she slowly unbuttoned his shirt and slipped it off his shoulders. What she could see so far she liked, he had a nice body. She placed her hands on his shoulders and used her fingers to tease him a bit. He followed her lead and when his hands were on her shoulders she traced his arms until she reached his hands. She took one and brought each finger to her lips so she could kiss those fingers, repeated the same to the other hand. He repeated her movements for her and again the room exploded with fireworks. For a fleeting moment she wondered what to do next but decided to do just what felt right.

She brought her hands back up his arms to his chest and slid them down gently teasing him along the way to his stomach. His smile let her know he approved of her movements. He followed her lead but lingered quite a bit longer than she had. She exploded on the inside and by the way she reacted, he knew he was well on the way to satisfying her.

Their exploration lasted for some time and while touching each other she had managed to completely disrobe him and he her. His touch was much like the silk that her gown was made from, soft, gentle yet purposeful and his kisses were intense. She knew that she wanted him and she could see that he wanted her. He laid her back against the pillows placing one under her hips. He didn't want to scare her so he took his time making love to her until he brought them to a climax together.

Not wanting to move he held her tightly and she did not want him to move either. What had just happened? She never dreamed it would be this good. She was so happy and relieved that she started to cry.

Sammie: "I didn't hurt you, did I?"

Suzie: "No, not at all, I'm just so happy."

Sammie: "Suzie, you are incredible. You felt so good and I loved the way you touched me."

Suzie: I like what you did to me. It felt good, it felt right, can we do that some more?"

Sammie: "Of course we can, we can do this as much as you would like."

They laid in bed, holding each other tightly until Suzie fell asleep safely and securely in Sammie's arms. After about two hours she roused which must have

52

awakened Sammie because he stirred. He smiled at her and asked if their first time together had been good. Suzie assured him it had been amazing but she had to take care of something and left him to use the rest room. When she returned she could not help but notice the devilish look he had on his face. Tilting her head as if to say 'what', he used his finger to motion her back to the bed and she slide in next to him as he raised his head up on his arm. He told her he was going to do some amazing things to her and he did not want her to touch him at all, reminding her that if he did something she was not comfortable with to simply tell him to stop. She told him that was fine but what if she wanted to touch him? He assured her there would be another time for that.

His touch was better than it had been before if that was possible as he covered every inch of her with his tender touch and soft lips. They lost count how many times he had her reach her heights but he was pretty sure when he was finished she was well satisfied and ready to go back to sleep. He was right, she was positively exhausted and every inch of her tingled. Her last thoughts were of how much she was really going to like this.

Waking up the next morning she found herself alone in bed but could smell the scent of the bacon permeating throughout the house. Quietly she slipped out of bed to use the rest room. When she returned she found Sammie sitting on the bed with a tray of food. Oh my, breakfast in bed, was he serious? After ingesting his previous attempt at culinary skills she was worried, however, there was no need for concern, his bacon and eggs were incredible. Served on a tray with a beautiful red rose in a vase and coffee that tasted as good as it smelled, they ate in relative silence but each was smiling like little kids.

Suzie: "Last night was pretty incredible. Is that what it should always be like?"

Sammie: "Yes, especially the first time but it should be amazing every time. Sex is a loving thing shared between two people who care deeply for each other and, Suzie, I really do care for you a lot. Slowly and little by little I am going to teach you to do things to me that I like and other things. We are going to learn to play and have fun and mostly enjoy every time we make love."

Suzie: That sounds fair since I really like everything you have done to me so far."

Smiling, Sammie told her he had a surprise for her but first..... He moved the breakfast tray and again, they reached heights that amazed her. If this was so good, why did anyone fight or get divorced. She wondered why he had gotten a divorce but she didn't ask. Savoring the moment while lying in his arms he told her they were going to take a shower and go somewhere. This excited her because she knew that was a difficult task since she was under age and they would surely be leaving town. They showered together which made Suzie feel a bit awkward, but she was learning and learning fast. While she was dressing, Sammie cleaned up the kitchen from his breakfast and dinner mess.

When she had finished dressing, she walked out to the living room where he asked if she was ready and she said she was. He went to her, kissed her with those incredible lips and carried her out to his car. She asked where they were going and he said it was a surprise as they drove out of town chatting non-stop. They went to a state park located about a half hour north of town. A safe place, she would be able to relax. Sammie parked the car, opened the door for her and retrieved a picnic basket, blanket and radio from the trunk.

It was a gorgeous day, sunny, warm and they felt on top of the world. Finding a secluded spot under a huge tree, Sammie spread out the blanket and they sat together listening to the soft music.

Sammie: "So, you enjoyed yourself last night and this morning? I told you I wanted it to be very special for you, it was for me."

Suzie: "It was more than special. I had no idea that sex could be so good."

Sammie: "I promise you that every time we are together it is going to be as good if not better than it was last night and this morning. As we get to know each other better, it will just get better."

Suzie: "What are we going to do when the boys are home? I mean, we can't just go off to the bedroom whenever we feel like it. This could be hard."

Sammie: "We'll figure it out. We just have to be quiet but I have some ideas and I don't want you to worry about that right now. No problems, this weekend is about us."

When Sammie opened the picnic basket Suzie noticed it contained several different kinds of cheeses, breads and crackers. There was also a bottle of wine, but only one glass. Sammie opened the bottle, poured about a half of glass of wine and handed it to Suzie. She looked at him inquisitively and he told her that he did not drink any longer. He told her that he always wanted to be at his best with her and since he had a previous problem with liquor had decided when he met her that he was not going to drink any longer. This made Suzie happy, she knew from family members that alcohol could make people nasty, she could not imagine Sammie being nasty.

Laying there in the sun with her head in his lap, Suzie wondered if things would always be this way with him. She only knew dates to be movies, bowling, hamburgers, school dances and other kid stuff. Was she really ready for this kind of relationship with a man who was actually old enough to be her father plus he had four kids, what were they doing? Why was he so interested in her anyway? She blinked her eyes open, saw him staring down at her and needed some reassurance.

Sammie: "You are so beautiful. How did I ever get so lucky to have found you?"

Suzie: "I was thinking the same thing. I feel so lucky to have met you but what do you want with someone my age. I'm a kid and you are a man, what are we doing?"

Sammie: "You are far from a kid, you are more of a woman than most women my age. We are doing what comes naturally. Does our age difference really bother you?"

Suzie: "In some ways it does. I don't know what you expect from me. You are older, you've been married and you have a son who is only a few years younger than I am. We can't go out because of the age difference and it just makes me wonder, that's all."

Sammie: "Suzie, age is just a number. You can't help who you meet and are attracted to. When we get a little older, the age difference will not seem so bad. I'm not that old and yes, I know it really seems strange right now but it won't be this way forever."

Suzie: "I guess so. I know I have always liked older guys anyway, guys my age tend to be jerks and I don't have the patience for that nonsense."

Sammie: "You are wise beyond your years, you just have to stop thinking so much and enjoy the moment. If this is meant to be, it will work just fine."

He leaned down and kissed her tenderly. She vowed to herself that she would stop analyzing everything and enjoy the times they would be able to spend together. The afternoon drew on and neither wanted it to end. One more night and she would have to go back to the hell she knew as home. If only she were a few years older.

They returned to the house chatting for the entire drive. Sammie had purchased their dinner the previous day which he just needed to heat up. It was a relief that she did not have to eat something he cooked again. She made a mental note to teach him how to make real Italian food, not stuff that comes from jars or cans.

Sammie: "I want you to do something for me please."

Suzie: "Sure, what is it?"

Sammie retrieved another gift from the bedroom, handing it to her to open, she was in awe. When had he done all of this? She opened it and inside was another negligee. This one was white, sheer, flowing and very feminine; it was absolutely beautiful. He certainly had exquisite taste. She liked being spoiled and if this was how he would treat her forever, then she was more than willing to stop worrying about the age difference.

He took her in his arms telling her that he wanted her to wear that while they ate dinner. She could go and change while he heated up their dinner. She smiled at him and went off wondering how she had gotten so lucky.

Chapter 9

Whatever he had purchased for dinner certainly smelled sensational and it made Suzie's stomach grumble. She took great care in getting ready for their dinner when she heard the soft music playing. As with many couples, their relationship was defined by certain songs and the wishes they put in the Big Dipper. She liked it and knew that with someone her own age, it would never be like this.

Returning to the living room she found Sammie leaning over the stereo playing with some of the records and she stood there in her gown smiling. As she watched him select records and she thought that even from the back he was a very handsome man. She wondered what he had in mind for the night and smiled at the thoughts as naïve as they were. When he turned around and saw her, he gasped.

Sammie: "Oh my God, you are an angel. You look absolutely stunning, beautiful and I still can't believe how lucky I am to have found you."

Suzie: "I feel pretty lucky myself. Are you going to spoil me like this forever?"

Sammie: "You better believe it, you deserve to be spoiled."

He walked to her, took her in his arms, kissed her with intense passion that made her want him right then and there. She would have to wait, dinner was ready. While they ate, they talked more of the previous night, inquiring if she had any questions or wanted to know anything. She simply did not have enough experience to know if she had any questions so she told him that she was fine and happy. Dinner was delicious, he cleared the table and was standing by the sink when she went to him. She turned him toward her, took his face in her hands and kissed him. That was the first time she had done that and he responded with appreciated approval. Breaking the kiss, he smiled and told her he had been waiting for that. She could feel the strength in his arms and the tenderness in his hands through the flimsy material of the gown. It felt so good to be in his arms. She felt protected, safe, happy, content, and she could not imagine being anywhere else.

They went into the living room, he told her that he was going to guide her hands to where he wanted her to touch him. As he did, the room exploded. She not only liked him doing sweet things to her, but his reaction to her touch sent shock waves coursing through her. He gently whispered in her ear something else he really wanted her to do. You want me to WHAT? He laughed at her reaction but assured her that as he had done to her, this was something that was even more intimate than actually having sex. She looked at him, smiled and said she would try but he would have to tell her how.

It was pretty evident that he liked what she was doing but what surprised her more was that she really liked doing it, she wanted to make him feel as good as he had made her feel the previous night. Her grandmother's words echoed through her. You be a lady on his arm and a whore in his bed. So, anything goes and I am supposed to keep my man happy, then if his reaction was any indication she certainly had accomplished that.

Sammie pulled her into his arms and twirled her around the room. He was amazed that she had taken to all of this so well, even though she was young, inexperienced and he was grooming her for the life together that he had envisioned. She was a willing student and that just made this whole process easier.

They collapsed on the sofa together and he held her in his arms. She was a special young woman and he was right where he wanted to be and that was the moment he realized that he was beginning to fall in love with her.

Sammie: "Suzie you are amazing. Wise men say only fools rush in, but I can't help falling in love with you. Take my hand, take my whole life too, for I can't help falling in love with you."

Suzie: "What? Isn't it a bit too soon for you to say that to me?"

Sammie: "It may seem quick, but I do know how I feel. You are beautiful, smart, sensual and for a very long time I have been wanting to find someone like you, and I have. I just hope that someday you will feel the same way."

His revelation stunned her and she did not know quite how to react to this, and Suzie's mind wandered to those ever present doubts. What were they doing? This man and this girl, it was all wrong, there were also kids involved, how was she going to deal with all of this? She had another year and a half before she was even legal, could they survive? She closed her eyes so she would not have to interact with him as every fiber in her being told her that this was not the right thing and it would not work, but there was something deep inside her that made her want to stay. He made her feel safe and comfortable and most importantly the trauma she had endured not long ago was fading, the long term affects would always be with her but he made her feel good about herself. How could she not at least like him. Sex was not just sex with him as it had been that horrible night, it was making love which made her feel like an incredible woman, was that so bad? She decided that for the time being anyway she would just go with it and see where they ended up, but there were the boys. How would she deal with them? They appeared to be good boys, she liked them so far but she liked kids in general. Was she ready to take them on? If they were going to stay together then the boys would have to like her and she them. The second part was easy, she already did like them. Oh dear, she really needed to stop thinking so much and accept what he had just told her because right now she had no intention of walking away.

Her eyes fluttered open at the touch of his hand on her cheek causing her to smile sheepishly noticing the look in his eyes. He was so handsome, how could she doubt her attraction to him. His smile told her what he wanted and she smiled back. He picked her up off of the sofa and carried her to the bedroom where for the next two hours he held her on a star. They did things to each other that took them to new heights and she could not believe how lucky she was. They fell asleep entangled in each other and content that they were exactly where each wanted to be.

He woke her gently. It was still dark but she knew by the way he touched her what was on his mind. She smiled broadly and responded with a passion that surprised even her. It seemed that each time they made love it was better than the last time, was that how it was supposed to be? Suzie never knew that it could be this good, how could she even consider not spending any time with him.

Chapter 10

When dawn broke, Suzie woke first and slipped from the bed quietly enough to not wake Sammie. She smiled as she looked at him sleeping. Where did you come from she wondered. She went to the bathroom and then went to the kitchen to make breakfast. She found sausage and all the ingredients for French toast and proceeded to prepare breakfast for them. She carried the tray into the bedroom and found Sammie sitting on the bed with a huge smile on his face.

Sammie: "There's my beautiful girl. Suzie last night was amazing and now you bring me breakfast in bed? How did I get so lucky? You are absolutely incredible."

Suzie: "I thought you might like to be spoiled a bit since you have certainly outdone yourself this weekend."

Sammie: "You better get used to it because I will spoil you rotten every chance I get."

Suzie: "I will hold you to that, my sweet."

She set the tray down on the bed as he pulled her to him and she could feel his hands through the sheer material of the negligee. She liked wearing these for him and it seemed to please him. Breakfast would wait for what he said was a "quickie". Well, if that was a quickie she liked those too and she told him so. He just smiled as they began to enjoy breakfast together. Suzie fed him a fork full of French toast, he reciprocated and they proceeded to feed each other until the food was consumed even though it felt silly, it also felt so right. After they finished eating, Suzie took the tray back to the kitchen. When she returned it was more than obvious what was on Sammie's mind. For just a moment she pretended that she did not understand and was not interested. Making a grab for her and pulling her onto the bed, he started to tickle her. Trying to get away and laughing hysterically Suzie finally succumbed to his advances. He was playful this time and it was refreshing that she did not have to worry about being too serious all the time and they could play. They did just that for the rest of the morning and into the afternoon. She wondered if he ever got tired of it, because she certainly didn't.

She wanted a shower so she went to the bathroom to take one. They would still have a few hours before she would have to return to hell. When she finished she went to find Sammie who was sitting in the living room and told her they had to leave to get the boys. They were supposed to stay another week but they were a bit much for his mom to handle for that long, so she wanted him to come and get them. Suzie told him she only had a few hours left, could he be sure to get to his Mom's house and back in time for her to get home? He assured her they could, so they left. Oh my, she was going to get to meet his mother and this made her nervous. What would she think of her son seeing someone so young? She was not aware at that time that his mother already knew about her.

When they arrived at his mother's house, Suzie realized it was not that far from her grandparent's house, about five minutes away. Sammie's mom was outside when they arrived, she looked like a lovely person, greeting her with a broad smile. She could hear the boys playing in the back yard and it was good to hear their voices. Sammie's mom came to her, gave her a hug and thanked her which caused Suzie to look at her inquisitively. She said, "Thank you for coming into my son's life. He hasn't been this happy in a very long time. You are good for him." Oh my, what was she to say to that. They were invited to stay for dinner but Sammie told her that they had to get back to his house and they would do that another time. He told the boys to get their things and they did. It was obvious they really did not want to leave but they complied like the well behaved boys they were.

The ride home was filled with the boy's chatter about what they had done the previous week. Suzie could sense that Sammie was not all that happy to have them back and she knew why. Their play time was over. She felt the same way, but she enjoyed being around the boys so she really didn't mind. He stopped at A&W to get something to eat and then they were back at his house which now seemed normal again. Sammie was a bit distant, Suzie inquired what was wrong and he told her that he had plans for one more time or two to the moon before she had to leave. Suzie laughed, there will be other times she assured him even though she did wonder how they were going to manage it with the boys at home. He told the boys to put their things away. When they did, Sammie took her downstairs and showed her an extra room. With a devilish grin on his face, he told her this would be their playroom when the boys were home. Shrugging, she said, "don't you think they will figure out what we are up to?" and they both laughed.

Sammie had taken her bag to her car before he came back to carry her down the stairs. They stood by the car discussing how difficult it was going to be for her to leave. They had gotten used to being together very quickly and the level of their intimacy had increased dramatically this weekend, they simply did not want to be apart. He gathered her up in his arms, held her as if his life depended on it as they kissed with intensity and all-encompassing passion.

Sammie: "I had such a wonderful weekend with you, Suzie. You are amazing and I will hold your touch close to my heart until we can be together again."

Suzie: "This is going to be very hard to be away from you. I've had all kinds of doubts about us because of our age difference but now those doubts are gone. This was an absolutely amazing weekend and I will never forget it. Thank you for the memories."

Sammie: "Nor will I, just remember that I am falling in love with you and we will figure out how we can be together again. And you are welcome but remember always that it was my pleasure. Maybe you can spend another weekend at Kim's before long. I may be able to take the kids to Mom's again at least for the weekend. It helps that she likes you."

Suzie: Let me see what I can work out. It's going to be adjusting my work schedule that will be a bit difficult because of summer school. I'll check it out when I get to work tomorrow."

Sammie: "Oh, Suzie, our bed is not going to be the same without you. I'll just have to keep your pillow warm."

Smiling, Suzie pulled his head to her and kissed him with every inch of passion she felt in her heart. She was going to miss him tremendously, keeping busy would help only a little. She reluctantly got in the car, slowly backed out of the garage and could see the sadness in his eyes as she pulled away from the house. She started to wonder how she got so hooked on him so quickly and was he really being sincere about the way he said he felt about her. After being violated as she had been, Sammie made her feel worthy and she found herself beginning to trust him.

Chapter 11

Arriving home she found the atmosphere was filled with tension and after the weekend she just had, she could not understand how two people that were married could fight the way her parents did. She knew things were bad so she just parked her car and started upstairs. Her father called out, asking if she had a good time and she responded that she had but her mother said nothing to her. Suzie went to her room, laid down on the bed and cried. This weekend had been utterly amazing and to come home to this was horrible. She did not know that anyone could feel so good being with another person. Sammie was an incredible lover although she didn't have anything to compare this to except what Kim had told her. She recorded the entire weekend in her diary before she drifted off to sleep, Sammie had worn her out.

Waking up, Suzie realized she was hungry so she went to the kitchen to get something to snack on. Bringing her food with her, she laid on her bed, reliving the events of this weekend. She was just in awe at how tender, caring and sweet Sammie had been. Because she was missing him so much, she started to wonder how they were going to manage being together with the limited time they would have. She worried that he would get tired of the stolen moments they would have to manage and not want to see her any longer. What would she do then? She was convinced that there would never be anyone like him that would come into her life and she also knew that every bit of 'them' was morally, ethically and just plain wrong. He had told her over and over what he had seen in her but she just could not get used to the idea that they were so many years apart. He had lived a life time as far as she was concerned, he had been in the service, out of the country, married and was a father. What did he see in her and what did he want with her? It was a question she would never get a good answer to.

There was still about five weeks left of summer school then two weeks off and she would be a senior. She would check her schedule at work for the weekend two weeks from now. It may not be for the whole weekend but some time together would be better than nothing. Sammie called her that evening and they talked a bit. It was obvious that Suzie was not in a good mood. Sammie was teasing her about that and asking what was wrong, then she told him what it was like when she got home and it was upsetting her which in turn upset him. Hardly containing her tears, she told him that it would be really difficult to spend much time together for the next couple of weeks and felt this wasn't fair to him. He assured her that everything was going to be fine and he knew what he was getting into when he walked into the store that day. This was comforting and the tears stopped as he reminded her of those very special moments this past weekend, just how much they meant to him and that he would forever hold them in his heart. Calming down she asked how old the boys thought she was. He told her that the topic had never come up and he just told them that she couldn't be there that much because of her job. That sounded logical, after all he was their Dad and knew how to handle them. Just before hanging up he sang, "Goodnight Sweetheart" to her until he finished the song. His crooning voice was fine, but she remembered when he sang in the shower and his voice was right there with his culinary skills. She smiled at the memory.

Getting back to school and work helped a bit but things at home were still bad, and she hated any time she had to spend there. Work went by quickly and most of the time they had her working nights which was not always good because she would not have much time to get to see Sammie this way. But he did stop by the store about every other day or so to see her on his way home from work. Their closeness was evident and Jean mentioned that to her one day. Suzie had grown close to Jean confiding in her about their situation and how things had changed over that past weekend. Jean had figured it out by the way Suzie had been bouncing around the store, telling Suzie to just keep going the way things were, time would go quickly and if it was right it would work for them. It just seemed that everywhere she turned for advice everyone was convincing her that this was a good thing and if it was meant to be, it would work. She kept wondering what was causing her to have doubts.

During the next weekend, they had her working early on Saturday and late on Sunday. She would at least be able to see Sammie on Saturday night. This time she did not use Kim as an excuse, she just said she was going to go to the movies, meeting some friends from school there and then getting something to eat. That gave her until about ten that night but her father told her to be home by midnight. Cool, a couple more hours.

As always when she arrived at the house, Sammie was waiting for her in the driveway. He carried her upstairs when she realized how strangely quiet it was. Sammie told her the boys were down the street at a friend's house. They ran to the bedroom. They would have a couple of hours without interruption and they took full advantage of that time. The thought of the boys coming home hung in the air which made things a little more exciting for them. Finishing their trip to the moon and back a couple of times, they quickly dressed, making it out to the living room with only moments to spare before the boys came charging in. They sat there laughing at themselves as the boys were their same old goofing around selves and went off to their rooms leaving Sammie and Suzie to the living room.

Suzie: "I'm telling you, they know what we are doing."

Sammie: "No they don't. How could they?"

Suzie: "Because I always knew when my parents were fooling around which wasn't that often. Kids are kids and I'm telling you that they know."

Sammie: "If you say so. Hey, did you know that I love you."

Suzie: "You tell me enough, so I guess I know, I'm just not ready yet."

Sammie: "It's okay, I told you I wouldn't pressure you."

They spent the next hour and a half just quietly talking until Suzie went to light up a cigarette. Sammie knew she smoked and she had smoked there previously but he did not like it. He made a comment and that led to an argument. Their first argument and it was over a stupid cigarette. He wanted her to quit, she told him she enjoyed smoking and didn't want to quit. The argument escalated a bit to the point that they were yelling at each other. Suzie said she thought it was time to leave. Sammie grabbed her by the hand and said that was not how to have an argument. They needed to resolve this issue before she left. Exasperated she sat back down on the sofa. Sammie moved to the coffee table. Shit, this was going to be serious.

> Sammie: "Suzie, smoking is so unattractive. You are too beautiful to be smoking, plus it smells awful."
>
> Suzie: "I will seriously try to quit. I just enjoy it. I don't know why, I just do."
>
> Sammie: "Please try because I don't like it at all."
>
> Suzie: "I promise to try."

That satisfied him and he pulled her to him for some more sweet kisses. Mm-mmm make up kisses, she wondered what make up sex would be like. She giggled to herself and it was time to go. When he carried her outside, they noticed again how brilliant the stars were. Of course, they made their wishes and their kisses would have to sustain her.

During their short time together, Suzie had noticed a subtle change in Sammie's demeanor. The argument about smoking was not the cause because she noticed this change prior to that. She thought back through the events of the evening and everything seemed fine when she arrived. Everything seemed perfect actually and their time together was amazing as always. Then it dawned on her that the change came when the boys had returned. He just seemed to be a little quick with his responses both to her and the boys. She started thinking back a bit further and remembered that the same thing had occurred the day they went to his Mom's house to get them. This made her wonder and she was going to have to pay closer attention, then the thought crossed her mind that it could just be his 'daddy mode'.

Chapter 12

The next weekend was supposed to be another weekend together but those plans had to change since the boys were already home. Sammie had told her that they were going to spend one more weekend with their 'nana' before school started and he asked if she could arrange something for then. She would definitely try since school was starting and she would be working more nights. Suzie was still concerned about the difference in Sammie when the boys were around and she talked to Kim's mother about that. Kim's mother reassured her that he probably did not want the boys to think they were too serious and think that they would be having a step-mother come into the picture. She urged Suzie to talk to Sammie about what she had noticed. Since Kim's parents were not going to be away for the weekend she needed to let Kim's mother know the plans. A cook out was planned for that Saturday so Sammie could at least meet Kim, Gary and Kim's parents. That was only fair since Kim's mother was willingly covering for her. She told Sammie about the invitation for the cookout and he was okay with that.

The time seemed to drag on but finally summer school was over. There were two weeks left and it would be the following weekend that they could be together again. Without much time to see Sammie, even though he did call her every night that they were not together, it was distressing. She really wondered if he was going to get tired of this and not want to see her any longer. Once a seed was planted in Suzie's mind it was difficult to get rid of it, but she would just have to talk to him again. Since her age issue required an extra amount of reassurance, she hoped he would understand. She did vow to not smoke the weekend they were together. That would please him.

The days were finally winding down to the weekend. Friday she packed and told her mother that she would see her Sunday. Kim and Suzie were going school shopping the next day. It was easy for Suzie to not come home with anything, she was very fussy about her clothes and often did not find anything suitable so she was not concerned about not bringing anything home. When Suzie arrived at Sammie's he was not home yet. He had to drive down to his Mom's after work to take the kids there and she was not sure when he would get there. She went to A&W to get something quick to eat because she was hungry. She just sat there daydreaming when a car pulled in next to her. It was Sammie. He asked what she was doing and she told him. He smiled and said he would take care of that situation. Sammie told her to go up to the house and he would follow her so she could park in the garage.

As always, he carried her up the stairs. She liked being fussed over like that and wondered if he had treated his wife that way. That was not going to be a subject of conversation since anytime his ex-wife was mentioned, called, or thought about, it put him in a foul mood. He set her down at the top of the stairs and told her to put her bag in the bedroom. Oh my, what's this? On the bed was a present. She sat on the bed and thought, man if this is what it was like to be an adult, be in a serious relationship, be in love or married, she seriously liked this concept. Knowing Kim was not quite treated in the same way bothered her because everyone should have someone in their lives like Sammie. She decided she was going to have to start reciprocating with little gifts for him. She opened the box and had to stifle her hysterical laugh because inside the box was a little black outfit, very little. She could hear him going through some records and decided that if this is what he wanted, then this is what he would get. Her grandmother's words echoed through her head again, be a lady on his arm, a whore in his bed. She was not too sure about what a whore did and with her limited experience she would just have to try to figure it out as she went but she did change into that little black outfit. She actually liked the way she looked in this skimpy little thing and figured he would too. Suzie had an idea, she looked in his closet and found an old bathrobe that she slipped on, messed up her hair, and walked out to the living room. Sammie's back was to her so she was able to step up on the coffee table and pose.

Sammie turned around and could not contain his laughter. The robe was huge on Suzie and he had expected her to be dressed in next to nothing. He laughed so hard he had to sit down on the floor, Suzie started laughing also even though for a moment she had tried to be serious. After a few moments, he went to her, lifted her off the table and just held her with all his might.

> Sammie: "Suzie, you are funny. I love you. Damn, you can even make this ratty old thing look good."
>
> Suzie: "I'm not funny, you obviously want to play so play we will."
>
> Sammie: "Let's see what is under this old thing."

He slowly undid the belt to the robe and let it slide to the floor. He took a step back and just kept looking her up and down.

> Sammie: "Suzie, you are absolutely beautiful. You are gorgeous, more woman than girl."
>
> Suzie: "It's going to take some time for me to get used to all these different things you want me to be and do. I only know what you have taught me so far."
>
> Sammie: "You're fine. We can't experience everything in a month, it will take time for me to have you feel comfortable with me doing what I really like to do."
>
> Suzie: "And just what is that? Should I be worried?"
>
> Sammie: "Absolutely not. Remember I told you if I ever do anything you do not feel comfortable with, just say no and that's the end of it. I know you are young but having all of these first experiences with you is amazing to me also."
>
> Suzie: "So, you are grooming me to be your sex toy?"
>
> Sammie: "No, I'm trying to teach you so you can experience what it is like to be with someone who loves you and who you love. There should be no secrets, and trusting each other is what it takes. I just don't want to do anything you are uncomfortable with. Are you okay in that outfit?"
>
> Suzie: "Well, when I first put it on, I felt self-conscious but if you like it then it's okay, I want to please you."

Sammie went to her and took her in his arms. His kiss was absolutely intense, extremely serious yet tender. At the moment Suzie knew she was beginning to fall in love with him, but was not ready to tell him just yet. She still had some questions and concerns she wanted to discuss with him but this was not the time. She wanted to know just what he had planned for her in this itty bitty outfit.

Scooping her up, he threw her over his shoulder, swatted her ass, and carried her to the bedroom with giggling emitting from both of them. He sort of just threw her on the bed and proceeded to have a quickie without even removing his clothing which was different and fun. They were still giggling when Sammie took her face in his hands and simply told her that she was amazing. It was obvious he liked this little outfit and she wondered where he was keeping the rest of the negligees he had purchased for her. She asked and he showed her the bottom drawer of the dresser where they were all neatly folded just waiting for her. Good, so now she could change into what she wanted at times.

The rest of the night they spent exploring each other and memorizing the places they liked to be touched. Somewhere around midnight they fell into exhausted sleep entwined in each other. Suzie woke up a couple hours later and wanted to laugh but did not want to wake him. He was snoring and it was so cute. She needed the restroom so she untangled herself from him gently and went to use it. When she returned he was wide awake smiling at her. She just started laughing and telling him that he snored. He threw a pillow at her and she grabbed it and hit him with it. A pillow fight ensued causing fits of laughter from both of them. She definitely was falling in love with him and wanted more than anything in the world to be able to be with him forever and not have to go back home. Someday she vowed.

Chapter 13

The next day they were going to Kim's house. This would be the first time that they all met and it was surely going to be interesting. She wondered how he would fit in with Kim, Gary, and her family. If only she could have him come to the house with her parents but she knew that could never happen. They stopped at the store on the way to purchase something for dessert. Suzie started getting nervous about this cook out because Kim's father knew her father quite well and she was worried that he would say something to her father about Sammie and oh man, she just did not want to have to give up seeing him.

Kim and Gary thought Sammie was cool. Kim told Suzie that he was really handsome causing Suzie to smile and say that she knew that. They had a really good time. Kim's parents liked him also and there was laughter and much conversation throughout the afternoon. Suzie was in the kitchen with Kim's mom and she told Suzie that Sammie was really handsome and it was very obvious that he adored her. She said, "Lay low until you turn 18 and then you can do what you want. Just make sure I know when I'm supposed to cover for you." This made Suzie feel better. Gary and Sammie hit it off well which was good, maybe they would be able to do some things together.

Going back to Sammie's was exciting. Suzie wondered what he had in mind for her that night. It was always interesting to be with him. On the way to the house, Suzie asked Sammie why he was so different when the kids were around. He told her that with kids you have to be careful, he wanted her to get to know them and have them get to know her and like her, but since they couldn't be together that often it was better that they didn't think they were as close as they were. Let them think you are just around for the time being. He also told her that since Sam had asked several times if she had a brother he didn't want him to say anything. Suzie understood, but she wanted to be able to spend time with the boys alone, doing things with them and Sammie said not yet, it was too soon, he was their dad so she would listen to what he said.

They arrived at the house and again, Sammie scooped her up in his arms and carried her upstairs. He put her down on the sofa and told her he had something for her. He went to the bedroom and came back with something folded up in his hand. He opened it and handed her a key. This is the key to the house, so if you ever come here and I'm not here just let yourself in. What? This was quite a big step Suzie thought as she took the key. Sammie also told her that there was a key hidden in the planter on the front porch. This made her feel more connected to him than ever. He also told her that if she needed some place to just get away, she was welcome to go there anytime.

Sammie went to the stereo to choose music while Suzie sat on the sofa toying with the key. This was something she had not expected and if he trusted her that much then this was getting serious, so quickly. How did he know how he felt? Was all this happening just because he was divorced and missed having someone in his life? Did he want someone around because of the kids? That she doubted because he did not ignore her when the boys were here, he was just a bit stern. God, she wished she didn't think so much.

The rest of the night was spent on the moon. She was positively convinced that Sammie was the person she wanted to spend the rest of her life with and no one would ever be able to come close to the way he made her feel. She fell asleep safely tucked in his arms and with a smile on her face.

Neither one woke until the sun brightened the room. Sammie stirred first waking Suzie immediately. She ran to the bathroom and came out to see him dancing around the hallway. Funny. She climbed back into bed not sure what they were going to do that day. When Sammie came back into the room, he climbed in bed next to her and gathered her in his arms.

> Sammie: "I know it's going to be very difficult for us to have much time together for a while. We are just going to have to seriously deal with this and be together when we can be."

Suzie: "It's going to be hard. I should be able to get away some Saturday nights after work but our nights together will surely be limited because the boys will be here also."

Sammie: "Yeah, they don't need to be here when you stay over. In time, but not now."

Suzie: "I don't want things to change. I want to be with you all the time."

Sammie: "I know you do and I want that too, but for another year or so it is just going to have to be what we can make it."

Suzie: "What happens if you get tired of this, you won't want me anymore?"

Sammie: "That will never happen. You are my special angel and I love you. We are just going to have to have patience. Get here when you can, we have the room downstairs, and maybe we can figure out a weekend here or there to be together. I've gotten used to having you around and I really love having you here. It will be hard, but we are worth it and we will make it work."

With that he kissed her lips and she responded, but this time, she slid under the covers and took him to the moon. He pulled her up and just hugged her with tears in his eyes and told her again that he loved her. She was still not able to get those words out. After all, she was 16 years old. What was this thing called love? All she knew is that after feeling the way she did after the rape, he made her feel good about herself, made her feel special and most importantly feel safe. Is that what love was? Did anyone know what it really was? All she knew was that she wanted to stay wrapped in his arms forever.

After a leisurely breakfast, they dressed and left to retrieve the boys. Suzie was a bit quiet on the way to his Mom's house and he asked why. She told him that she wondered what his mother and father were thinking of this. He assured her that his mother thought the world of her and the boys really liked it when she was around, that was all that mattered. When they arrived at his mom's house, they were told they were staying for dinner. Sammie had told her that his mother was an exceptionally good cook. Suzie felt a bit unsure of his father because he just sat there staring at her, more like glaring which unnerved her.

Driving home with the boys, Suzie asked why they were so quiet. They told her that school was starting soon and they did not want to go back. What kid does? Suzie wanted to so that the year would be over quickly. They chatted a bit and arrived home just in time for Suzie to leave to go home. The boys asked why she was always leaving. Since they did not know how old she was, she simply said that she had to get ready for the work week and they seemed to accept that. She mentioned to Sammie how she felt about his father glaring at her. He told her to not worry about him.

Going home was agonizing for her. She knew that her parents were having serious issues again and it was not fun being at home. How she wished she could have Sammie come over and her parents accept him as Kim's accepted Gary. When she got there she was asked what she had found shopping and she said nothing. She was going to have to go out during the week to pick up some things for the school year. At that moment, she really didn't care, she wanted to be with Sammie, and not here so she just went to her room. This was going to be hard.

Chapter 14

School and work filled many hours but Suzie missed Sammie and it was pretty obvious that Sammie missed her because he was stopping by at work every night that she worked. She tried to get over to his house whenever she could and they would slip away to the room in the basement. It was good to be together but seeing each other as they were right then seemed to cheapen their relationship and neither of them liked it. Their moods were not the best and they could sense the frustration building in each other. The holidays were coming and they knew that they would have to spend them apart this year which broke both of their hearts. On one of the rare occasions that Suzie was able to stay at the house for more than an hour or so, they decided that they needed to have a serious discussion. The boys were told to stay in their rooms and Sammie took his place on the coffee table. Suzie really hated that table.

He was trying to be positive and Suzie knew this. Her age and lack of maturity reared its ugly heard.

Suzie: "I really want things to be the way they were during the summer. I hate this and it makes it so much worse when I have to go home."

Sammie: "Suzie, we have to be patient, you know that. It's only a little more than a year and then we will be together forever. We are worth the wait."

Suzie: "It's the waiting that's really hard. Aren't you getting a little frustrated with me not being able to be here often?"

Sammie: "Yes, it is hard and I want so much to be with you more than you know. The time we spent together during the summer is burned in my memory and we are just going to have to depend on those sweet memories to get us through this. We knew it was going to be hard."

Suzie: "I don't know if I can do this. Things at home are horrible. They don't even talk to each other anymore, they always fight about my curfew, what my mother cooked for dinner, everything. I don't know if I can handle much more of all this. I just want to walk away from all of that and be here with you and the boys."

Sammie: "I know baby, I wish I had an answer for you. All we can do is look forward to the moments we are able to take advantage of right now. The boys have been asking about why you haven't been around that much."

Suzie: "What are you telling them so if they ask me I can tell them the same thing?"

Sammie: That you are really busy with work and school and you get here when you can."

Suzie: "I guess that will have to do, you know best when it comes to them."

Sammie: "I thought you were going to quit smoking? I smell it on you."

Suzie: "Don't start with that and don't start telling me what to do."

Sammie got mad and it started. First the words flew. Suzie, lacking experience in situations such as this, started to leave and that's when Sammie threw the ashtray at her. It didn't hit her but she was stunned. Suzie's temper flared and she threw a small statue at him which escalated to where they were throwing dishes and anything else they could grab. Her aim was deadly and she managed to hit him a few times, which stunned him. One of the neighbors heard this fight and had called the police. When the officer arrived at the house, it was a neighbor of Suzie's. Sgt. Devane entered the house to calm the situation down. When he saw Suzie it was evident that he was surprised and asked if her parents knew she was there. She told him that they knew where she was. She was not aware at that time that Sammie was well known to the local police. They calmed down and Sgt. Devane escorted Suzie to her car and told her to not come back until they could solve issues without fighting. This was not good, now she had to worry about him telling her parents.

Suzie left and went to the back side of the lake, her thinking spot. She wasn't sure she could take much more of this frustration which mostly involved the situation at home which made her want to be with Sammie that much more. What was she doing with him anyway, he deserved someone he could see whenever he wanted and not have to deal with the childish games. Even though he said he was

80

patient and seemed to be very understanding Suzie could not help but wonder how long that would last. The holidays were coming and they used to be very special, spent with extended family, but the last few years were horrible. This year she feared it would be worse especially since she could not see Sammie. With the prospect of having to go home, she tried to calm down. She certainly could not walk into the house with a blotchy face and tears flowing. What was she going to do?

She decided to go and get something to eat, this way she would not have to spend another tense dinner at the house. A&W seemed to be the go-to place so that's where she went. While she sat there eating she was trying not to think of Sammie, less than a mile away. She was going to have to curb her temper because they certainly did not need the police going to the house again. The fight was not like what happened at home but it was still their first really big fight. Was this going to be the end of them? Only time would tell, until then she would just have to keep going on with work and school.

Her suspicions were confirmed when she arrived home. Her brother told her that they had been fighting all afternoon and early evening. Suzie just wanted to get back in her car and leave but she couldn't do that. She had the next day off from everything and was going Christmas shopping with Kim and this time that was the truth. It was a week day and Sammie had to work so it might be a good thing to be away from him for a couple of days. The holiday season was not going to be fun at all. On her way to her room, she heard the phone ring. Since her parents were still at it, she went into her parents' room to answer the phone. It was Sammie. He was quite upset and asked where she had been. What:? Now he was checking up on her? He told her that he had driven over to her house and did not see her car there and he wanted to know where she was. She told him what she had done, but he was still upset and wanted her to come back to the house to discuss their argument, but she would not be able to do that. It would be almost a week before she could get over there again.

Suzie: "See, I told you this wasn't going to work. You are going to get tired of us not being able to see each other when we want. I want to be with you, I'm frustrated, angry and upset."

With that she hung up the phone and decided that they would just have to wait to talk. Going into her room she wondered how someone older would handle the situation. What did she know at 16? The phone rang again but she did not answer it, she needed time to think. There was too much going on, maybe she shouldn't have gotten involved with him. The age difference alone was going to cause problems, she could see that now. So far they had been lucky to have not gotten caught but that couldn't last, things like this never did. With all of this frustration weighing heavily on her, she went to her room, shut the door, laid down on the bed and cried herself to sleep.

The next day she was able to talk everything over with Kim. Kim was driving so Suzie had no control over where they were going. Kim told her that she had to make things right with Sammie and stop the ridiculous arguing which did seem quite silly after a night to cool off. There really was not much they could do about how often they could see each other, but they could come up with a plan to make it a bit easier. With that thought planted in Suzie's head, Kim drove to where Sammie worked. Suzie could see him pacing behind the building as they pulled into the parking area. As soon as he recognized Kim's car, he ran over to greet Suzie, grabbing her by the hand and led her to the storage room, telling Kim to wait a bit.

Sammie: "Suzie, are you alright? I spent the entire night last night trying to figure out how we could make this easier for both of us."

Suzie: "Sammie, I'm sorry. My frustration is at the point where I don't know how much more I can handle. I want to be able to see you like we could during the summer, I want things to be that way between us, not fighting. I'm a kid, I don't know how to handle this grown up stuff."

With that, Sammie started laughing.

Sammie: "Oh baby, you are doing fine. I should have never shown you my temper. I'm sure that scared you and that is something I don't ever want to do."

He pulled her into his arms and she instantly felt better.

Sammie: "There is nothing you can do about your parents' issues. The only thing we can do is be there for each other and do the best we can about seeing each other. Even an older woman would have difficulty dealing with a situation like ours. Look at me, I started throwing things and I am so very sorry I did that. The last thing I ever wanted to do was to scare you. I love you."

Suzie: "I don't know if I can handle not seeing you. That is harder than having my parents fight all the time. I hate it, it's horrible at home. The only good thing I can see about our situation is that with me not being able to get out so much, they don't think I'm seeing you much, if at all. But I still hate it and I am so frustrated."

Sammie: "We really need to sit down and talk this out. I don't have much time right now and you and Kim need to go shopping. Can you manage to get over to the house this weekend either before or after work?"

Suzie: "I think I can figure something out for Saturday night. I get off at 3 I'll see if I can go to Kim's house. I can't stay over there because I have to work early on Sunday."

Sammie: "Good, because we really need to come up with a plan that will work for us. Just remember I love you and I hate seeing you like this."

He gave her a quick kiss and she felt a little better. Time would tell and now she couldn't wait until Saturday. Getting back into Kim's car she was ready to shop. Kim was relieved to see her smiling and asked how they were going to handle the situation. Suzie told her that she was going to his house on Saturday so they could have a serious discussion. Kim smiled and told her that was the way to handle disagreements, not throwing things.

Chapter 15

Finally, it was Saturday, work went by quickly, and it usually did on Saturdays. Suzie was able to get off at two instead of three and she called Sammie to let him know. He seemed happy to hear that but he was quite quick on the phone with her which perplexed her but she would know what was going on soon.

She drove to Sammie's house and as always, he was standing in the driveway waiting for her. He had pulled his car out of the garage and motioned for her to park her car in the garage. This had been working fine in case her father had decided to check up on her. Getting out of the car, she found herself being pulled into Sammie's arms, her favorite place to be. Just being in his arms made everything seem right and that it would be right again.

> Sammie: "Oh baby, I love you so much. I am so sorry for losing my temper and throwing things at you. That was more childish than anything you could come up with and having the cops come to the house was not a good thing."

> Suzie: "I know Sammie. I was and still am concerned that Sgt. Devane will say something to my parents. He lives right behind us."

> Sammie: "I know. We have to make sure we don't do anything like that again, besides you don't need any more stress."

> Suzie: "It's simple. I just want to be with you, have a quiet and normal life. I am so sick and tired of my parents fighting, that's all they do and when we don't get along I feel like you are going to tell me you don't want to see me any longer and want someone who can be here for you."

> Sammie: "Oh Suzie, is that what's been worrying you? There is no one I would rather be with than to be with you. Suzie, I love you, I cherish you, and I always want you to feel safe with me."

> Suzie: "Well I don't feel that way right now."

> Sammie: "Let's go upstairs and talk this through. The boys are down the street and we have a couple of hours before they come home. I'm making dinner so we can all eat together."

That was a new concept. He scooped her up in his arms and carried her upstairs. She thought for a moment they would go to the bedroom, but not so, he sat her down on the sofa. There was no music playing and she waited for him to sit on the damn coffee table but he did not. He sat next to her on the sofa, turned to face her and took her hands. She knew then that this was going to be a serious discussion but she was glad he had not sat on the table.

Sammie: "First of all, I don't ever want you to forget how much I have come to love you. There is no one else I would rather be with, no one else I want to love and I am going to prove to you that I can patiently wait until you turn 18. I want you here and yes, I want things to be like they were this summer and they will be again, right now we have some obstacles to overcome. We are worth the wait and the difficulties we are going to face."

Suzie: "Sammie, I care a great deal for you. It's so hard to remember our good times when I go home to the fighting and arguing which seems to be all the time now. I'm trying to be patient and be good, it's just so hard when I really want to be here with you. I don't know how to handle all this, and this is when I really feel like just a kid."

Sammie: "Oh baby, you are more than a kid, you are more than most women ten years older than you. We are going to work out a plan and make this work so you don't have any more doubts. You just have to promise me that any time you have any concern that you will talk to me about it so we can work it out."

Suzie: "I promise."

Sammie: "Now, Christmas is coming soon and we both know that we can't spend any of the holiday together. Not eve Thanksgiving. It's going to be difficult but I have a plan. I will be taking the boys to Mom's for Thanksgiving and Christmas. I am going to leave them there from Christmas until that Thursday. You don't have school so maybe you can stay at Kim's for a night or so and we can be together. I know this year is going to be the hardest thing for both of us and you have to promise me that there will be no gifts for either of us and I don't want you to spend any money on the boys either. I know you want to and under different circumstances I would say sure, but let's just leave it with no gifts. Besides you are gift enough for me."

Suzie: "I really wanted to at least get something for the boys but what you are saying makes sense so I guess you are right. I think I will be able to get at least a couple of days off so we can spend time together. What I'm going to do this time is take my car up to Kim's and leave it there. You will have to come up there to get me."

Sammie: "That is a good idea and yes I will certainly come and get you. At least this way you can say that you and Kim were off doing stuff or out with her mother if anyone checks. Oh baby, I know this is so hard but it's worth it and trust me, when the time comes I will prove to you just how much you mean to me."

Sammie took Suzie in his arms, he just wanted to hold her and she was right where she wanted to be. He was so much wiser than her, this was going to work, Sammie said so. They still had an hour or so before the boys were due to come home so Sammie carried her into the bedroom. Their intimacy was something that would astound most anyone. He was so kind, gentle, loving and easy to be with when everything was right. She was going to have to believe that everything would be as he said. There was that trust issue again. She realized then that this was what was causing all the doubts. She was still having difficulty trusting.

The boys showed up right on time which always amazed Suzie at how well-behaved these two were. She was really starting to enjoy being around them. Sam was still a bit quiet but having a brother the same age she knew that this was common for an almost teenage boy. Teddy on the other hand continued to be quite the chatterbox. Sammie had to tell him to settle down more than once. Teddy always seemed to hang around her more than Sam did and that was fine. She really did like the boys and couldn't wait until she could do things with them.

Sammie's culinary skills left a lot to be desired but they all ate dinner with enthusiasm. She thought to herself that one of these days, she would cook them one of her meals. After helping to clean up the kitchen that looked as if a bomb had gone off in, it was about time to leave. She always hated this part, but felt much better this time. Sammie was right, it was going to work and she was going to do her part to make sure it did.

Chapter 16

The next month was tough. They saw each other when they were able to. Suzie was counting the days until she could spend the night with him again and it was only just before Thanksgiving so she had a little over a month to wait. She asked for more hours during the holiday season because it would make it easier to deal with not being able to see Sammie much. Her bosses were glad to accommodate her and added hours to her schedule, besides if she requested more hours before Christmas they would be a little better about giving her a couple of days off after.

At work, Jean was a savior. Suzie had told her about Sammie and all the issues. Jean was always very supportive even though she also thought the age difference could be a problem. She helped Suzie with some questions she had about dealing with those issues. Besides Sammie and Suzie, Jean knew more about the situation than anyone else did. There were just some things that she could not share with Kim because their fathers knew each other. Jean was teaching Suzie more make-up techniques when one day a woman entered through the back of the store. She was dressed exquisitely with a lot of jewelry and furs. Jean recognized her right away. It was Estee Lauder, the owner of a vast make-up company and a dear friend of Jean's. Suzie was introduced to her and was quite excited about meeting her. They talked for a long time while Jean showed her around the make-up section of the store. Jean also shared photographs of women Suzie had made up for special events. Estee told her that she had quite a talent and did an excellent job. She encouraged Suzie to consider a future in the business and offered to let her tour her school in New York City. Suzie said she would consider it.

The days dragged on and finally Thanksgiving was over. Dinner that year consisted of all of the traditional foods and the grandparents that were so dear to her were present in Martin's Cove. Her father's mom was also there and she adored her also. Holidays used to be such fun when they lived in Petersville, now they were mundane and usually filled with arguing. At least this year it was quiet but the tension in the household was quite profound. After dinner was over, her father and mother had to take her grandmother back home and Suzie did not want to go, but Joe did. After they left, she called Kim and talked with her for a while and then called Sammie to see if he was home from his Mom's yet. He had just gotten in so the timing was good. They talked on the phone for quite a long time. Everything seemed to be going as Sammie said it would and they both knew that they had something to look forward to in about a month.

After their conversation, Suzie went to her room and put on some music. She decided that she was going to bring some of her records to Sammie's house. She liked Elvis Presley but Sammie only had one of his records. She liked the music he had except for one that she did not care for, an album by Don Ho. Sammie liked the song "Tiny Bubbles", Suzie did not. She did like when Don Ho sang "I'll Remember You", but she liked Elvis' version a lot better. She wondered what it was about Don Ho that he liked.

Since her work schedule had been increased, she was scheduled to work the next three days almost all day and that was fine. She arranged to go up to Kim's house that Saturday night for a little bit after work. Sammie seemed happy to hear that she could get there that weekend. Spending the holiday apart had been really difficult. Then she thought for a moment, what about New Year's Eve? She wanted more than anything to bring in the New Year with the man that was seriously winning her heart. There was a party at one of Kim's cousin's house but she was not going to be able to bring Sammie there because they all knew her parents and if this was going to work then they had to keep a low profile. Gary said she could go with his brother and that would make her father happy. Her father was beginning to give her a hard time about how much she was seeing Sammie, he felt he was too old for her. Suzie would have to discuss this issue with Sammie and knew that he was not going to like it any more than she did.

For the next couple of weeks, it was busy at school and at work. Suzie had mentioned to Sammie about going to the party with Gary's brother. He did not like that at all as she had predicted and told her that they would discuss it when she was there after Christmas. This was just not right and she hated to have to do this but she still had a little over a year to go before she was 18.

Jean had mentioned to her at work one day that Estee Lauder really wanted her to attend her school in New York City. She also mentioned that she would be able to stay in Estee's apartment while going to school which would keep the costs down and give her quite a career. Suzie liked doing make-up but wasn't sure if she wanted to do it all the time. She told Jean that she would seriously start thinking about it. Jean reminded her that she had been invited to tour the school at her convenience.

There were so many things to think about. In the next six months, she would be graduating from high school. Her mother was pushing her to enroll in Berkeley Secretarial School. Even though she was taking business classes in high school, that was the last thing she wanted to do. She really did not like that kind of work. She had been appointed the Sports Director's assistant to keep her from being too bored but she hated typing letters and taking short hand. Kim was going to attend Berkeley and that did not help with Suzie's mother. There was also Estee Lauder's offer to consider which she wasn't sure she would be allowed to be in the city alone since she was only going to be 17. There was just too much to think about at the moment and with Christmas only a week away, she just wanted to think about being with Sammie.

Chapter 17

Christmas Eve was very difficult. Thankfully, Suzie had to work until six that night. Going home would be torture since she wanted to see Sammie but they had decided to just wait for a few days. He had been stopping at the store most nights on the way home but that only served to make Suzie miss him even more. Aren't people who love each other supposed to be together at special times? Oh my, what had she just thought? "People who 'love' each other?" Did she love Sammie? Thinking back on the last six months of their lives, she decided that yes, in fact she did. Did she really know what love was at 16? The one thing she did know for sure was that she did not like the way she felt when they were not together. She loved the way he touched her, kissed her, talked with her, solved problems with her and with the exception of throwing things, she even liked the way they argued. She decided that she was in love with him and that was going to be her gift to him for Christmas, her heart.

Christmas was okay, there was no fighting but there wasn't much to smile about either. After the gifts were opened, her father went down to the garage, her mother to the kitchen. She just sat in the living room wondering when this was all going to end. Were her parents going to get themselves back together or get a divorce? She really wanted them to be more like Kim's parents. She knew her father could if he had the chance, but her mother was another story. It seemed the angrier her mother got with her father, the more she took it out on Suzie. Oh God, please make this next year go quickly. Suzie went to the kitchen and asked if she could help with dinner and was told no. Her brother, Joe, was in the garage with her father and she did not want to interrupt their time together so she went to her room to be alone. Two more days and they would be together. It was only that thought that made dinner and the rest of the day tolerable. Later in the evening, Kim called with great news, Gary had asked her to marry him. Suzie was so happy and excited for Kim. Yes, it hurt, but Kim was her best friend and she was genuinely happy for her. They were going to have lots to do because Kim had asked her to be her maid of honor. Oh, this would be fun and maybe help make the next year go by quicker.

A few minutes later, Sammie called to wish Suzie a Merry Christmas. He knew right away that something was wrong and asked about it. Since they had talked about not having any secrets between them, Suzie shared that Christmas was at least without a fight, she wanted to be with him, and that Kim and Gary had gotten engaged. He knew instantly that Suzie was wishing that it was her with a ring on her finger. He talked gently, telling her about his day at his mother's, sharing that his brother had been there and since they did not get along well it wasn't a great day. He also shared that his parents had asked about her and wondered when they would see her again. The boys were excited to be at Nana's house and they had a fairly good Christmas. Suzie could hear that there was something off in his voice, she knew right away what it was. She asked him if he had talked to Cara and Jack. She heard his voice crack when he said he had called twice and was told both times that the kids were busy and he would have to call back. She needed to see him and told him she would be over in a few minutes.

She told her parents that she was going to Kim's house to see the ring that Gary gave her and that was a good excuse to get out of the house for a bit. Suzie drove to Sammie's but he was not in the driveway. That was fine, she knew that he was sad about not talking to Cara and Jack. She let herself in and found him on the sofa in tears. It was obvious that he loved his kids so much and with the boys not being there it was even harder on him. Suzie went to him, held him and let him cry which broke her heart. She suggested he try to call them now. He did and finally was able to talk to them. He had calmed down by the time he returned to the living room. Suzie always gave him privacy when he was talking to the other kids. She knew that if it were her kids, it would be tearing her heart into pieces and she knew Sammie felt the same way.

After asking about Cara and Jack, it was apparent that his mood was still dampened. She certainly could understand that and just held him. She got up from the sofa and moved to the coffee table. This had become a bit of a joke between them because when one of them sat on the coffee table it was always time for serious conversation. Suzie took his face in her hands and looked into his eyes.

> Suzie: "I know this is a really hard time for you and this is probably not the best time but I wanted to tell you something."
>
> Sammie: "What?"
>
> Suzie: "I know we said that we would not get each other gifts and I listened, but I do have something I want to give you."
>
> Sammie: "What's that?"
>
> Suzie: "I want to give you my heart. Sammie, I love you."
>
> Sammie: "What did you say?"
>
> Suzie: "Sammie, I love you."
>
> Sammie: "Oh Suzie, do you have any idea how long I have been waiting to hear you say that? That is the best gift you could have ever given me. I accept your heart and will cherish it forever. I will protect it, keep it from harm, and always love you."
>
> Suzie: "Oh Sammie, I do love you even more than I thought."

With that said, he rose and pulled her to him, his arms around her felt better than ever. How could this be so right yet be all wrong at the same time? The kiss they shared was precious and one that she would never forget. There was something special between them, something that could not be put into words. Yes, it all may have been wrong, but it was also so right, positively magic.

> Sammie: "I know how you feel about Kim getting a ring. Suzie, trust me, when the time is right we will be able to share a ring also."
>
> Suzie: "I know, it's just hard but we have already had this conversation and I don't want to spoil this moment right now. I love you, I love you, I love you."

He scooped her up and twirled her around the room. They knew they did not have much time, but in a couple of days they could spend a night together and he vowed to himself to make this special, more special than ever before.

Sammie: "I love hearing you tell me that you love me."

Suzie: "Well, I do. I'm not sure I really know what love is or if anyone really knows what it is but I know what it isn't. I do not like being away from you, I like the way your arms feel around me, I like the way your kisses feel, and when we make love you make me feel so special and I decided that I do love you. Not only that, it really scares me to even think about what it would be like if you were not in my life."

Sammie: "Oh baby, because you waited to tell me it just makes it more special. I love you, too and I don't ever want you to forget it."

Suzie: "I won't as long as you don't forget I love you either."

Their kiss sealed the fact that the feelings between them were genuine and as strong as they could ever be in that moment. Everything was right, not just right, their world was perfect.

Suzie had to leave, which was difficult. She was still concerned about his agony over Cara and Jack and she really did not want to leave him alone. He told her that he would be okay and for her to go up and see Kim's ring so she could tell the truth about seeing it and they would see each other again in two days. Two days, God that seemed like an eternity.

Kim and Gary were really excited, as were her parents. The ring was pretty and it looked perfect on Kim's hand. Suzie seriously had to contain her envy but she was genuinely happy for them. It was just so wonderful and there were no plans yet except that Kim had decided to definitely attend Berkeley and the wedding would be after she graduated. There was a lot of excitement and it was obvious that Kim's parents were happy for her. They were going to have fun making plans for this great event.

Chapter 18

The next two days did go by quickly. Sammie had called her the night before and told her that he had arranged for the next two days off so they could spend this time together uninterrupted. Suzie had made arrangements to leave her car at Kim's house. Kim was home so they talked for a while until Sammie showed up. Sammie made the appropriate comments about Kim's ring and all the plans. When Kim told him that they would be getting married after they graduated from Berkeley and Suzie would already be 18, he said that it would be great to finally make public appearances with Suzie.

They left to return to Sammie's house or so Suzie thought. Instead, Sammie drove south of town taking her to an Italian restaurant he had heard about. He wanted pizza and that was fine with Suzie, she liked pizza. They enjoyed their meal, talking of the holidays that had just passed. She knew that she was going to have to discuss New Year's Eve with him, but he was in a good mood and she did not want to change that. She knew that he was not happy about it and he knew she was not either but it was just one more thing they would have to endure to reach their destiny.

After enjoying the pizza, they drove to Sammie's house. He pulled the car into the garage and came around to open the door. As Suzie started to get out of the car, he reached down and scooped her up. No prelude, he took her straight to the bedroom. As he set her down, he whispered in her ear that he wanted to slowly undress her and he wanted her to watch him in the mirror, she simply smiled.

It seemed that every time they were together it was always better than the previous time. By the time they were finished, Suzie was totally exhausted. She started to doze off but Sammie told her that he had some serious things he wanted to talk to her about.

Suzie: "Oh God, not the coffee table again."

Sammie: "No, we're going to talk right here."

Suzie: "Okay."

Sammie: "First of all I want you to know that I love you silly. Shh, don't say anything until I finish. I know you are at least a bit jealous of Kim and Gary's engagement. It will happen for us too, but our circumstances are different from theirs so we just have to be patient. I've been giving this a lot of thought. I know you are going to want a wedding but under the circumstances that will be difficult to plan let alone pull off. So, on your birthday, when you turn 18, we are going to just leave. We are going to go to Las Vegas to get married. No one will be able to stop us and you will be legal. Then we are going to take a cruise to the Caribbean. This way no one will bother us because only Kim will know where we are. I talked to my mother and she is willing to come up here for that week so the boys won't miss any school."

Suzie: "You have been doing some thinking. Are you sure that's how you want to do it?"

Sammie: "Yes, it will just be the two of us and we will make it special."

Suzie: "Are you asking me to marry you?"

Sammie: "Not yet, I just wanted to let you know about the plans I've been thinking of. This way no one will get in our way and by the time we get back, it will be too late. You will be 18 and there won't be anything anyone can do about it. You will then be my wife."

Suzie: "Oh Sammie, that sounds like a perfect plan. 15 months seems like forever though."

Sammie: "It does and I know that we are going to have some trying times between now and then but I just want you to know that I've been thinking really hard about this and that's what I want."

Suzie: "Well, in that case yes, it sounds like a good plan. But, wouldn't you want the boys there?"

Sammie: "Suzie, they have school and I don't want them to miss that much. Yes, I would love for us to have all of our families there to celebrate but you know that will be impossible. Your father alone will give you a hard time, so if we are married when we get back there won't be anything he or your mother or anyone for that matter can do about it."

Suzie: "This is true. I don't care about a big wedding, it will be our wedding and will be special for us. I could at least get something special to wear that day. Could we stay in Las Vegas the first night? I really would like that first night to be just us."

Sammie: "I thought of that too and yes, we can stay in Vegas that night and then we will fly to Florida for the cruise. How does that sound to you? And now, does that make you feel a little better about us?"

Suzie: "Sammie, I never felt bad about us but yes, as long as we can survive the next 15 months, then yes, it sounds like a good plan. I love you."

Sammie: "And I love you."

Well, that did make Suzie feel better even though she could not say anything to anyone yet. The plans they had between themselves were something to look forward to. But oh, the next 15 months would be torture. If only Suzie knew what was in store for her.

Of course, that night and the following day went too quickly. They were so good together and they knew it. All the doubts she had about how he felt about her seemed to dissolve over time and she knew that she loved him with all of her heart. They both knew that the circumstances of their relationship were wrong on all levels, because of their age difference, however, he came into her life at a time when her world had been turned inside out and he made her feel good about herself, safe, loved and happy. How could it be wrong?

Chapter 19

The next couple of months were almost unbearable and Suzie just kept thinking about their plans. They were used to spending a lot of time together and with school, work, her parents and the boys being home it was difficult to even enjoy a few minutes together alone. Suzie wanted to spend more time with the boys. She really needed to get to know them better and they needed to get to know her if she was going to become part of this family. She wondered about Cara and Jack, would she ever get to know them, as she wanted to. They were supposed to be coming for a month this summer and the boys were supposed to spend that month with their mother. Sammie had not shared much about his ex-wife and Suzie did not ask. She knew that in his own way he still cared for her, after all, she was the mother of his children. But she knew only what he said about her and she just decided to not form any opinion. Whatever the reason, they were not able to make their marriage work and now he was hers. She did not need any further explanations.

Her birthday was approaching and for the first time in a long time, she looked forward to it. She would be all of 17 and would now start counting the weeks until the following year. Sammie had asked if she could stop by on her birthday. She told him she could do better than that. She had arranged to have that night off from work and was going to spend the night with Kim. She was off that Sunday also. This way they could be together and that would be the best birthday she could think of.

Jim and Carol were fighting so much now that they hardly noticed what was going on around the house. Suzie had told them of her plans for her birthday and they said that was fine. They could have a family dinner on Friday night. That was going to work because she would be getting out of work at six that evening. It was obvious on that night that something was really going on at the house but she didn't care. They had their own problems and she had enough to deal with juggling all of this scheduling. They had a cake and of course she received money for her birthday which was fine, she could always use the money.

Suzie woke the next morning excited. She knew there would be no gifts from Sammie and that was fine, how could she explain that. There would be time for that a year from that day anyway. Sammie had taken the boys to his Mom's the day before and she did not understand why but if that's what he wanted, then that was fine. She dressed quickly and threw some stuff in her bag to leave. She said goodbye to her mother who was in the kitchen and was told to have a good time. Going out through the garage she saw her father who wished her a happy birthday again and told her to have fun. She said she would, she and Kim had some wedding plans to discuss and the fact that they were both going to be attending Berkeley in the fall. Her father just smiled as she left.

As she drove to Sammie's she wondered how much her father really knew. He acted like he knew more than he was willing to let on but he said nothing. This was a worry she put in the back of her mind as she pulled into the driveway and her sweet Sammie was standing there waiting for her. He always seemed to know what time she would arrive. She pulled into the garage, opened the car door to find him standing right there.

> Sammie: "Happy Birthday, my sweet Suzie. I can't sing '16 Candles' for you anymore, can I now?"
>
> Suzie: "Nope, and one year from today you will be my husband."
>
> Sammie: "Better yet, you will be my wife."
>
> Suzie: "I am going to live this entire year waiting for that day."

He scooped her up in his arms and made his way slowly up the stairs. There were rose petals everywhere, flowers all over the living room, candles lit, and 'Happy Birthday, Baby' playing on the stereo continually repeating. She could not contain herself, she hugged and kissed him. She couldn't thank him enough that everything was so beautiful. Now she knew why he took the boys to his mother's. The song finished and Sammie took her to the sofa. Instead of sitting on the coffee table, he kneeled down in front of her.

Sammie: "I know we talked about not doing gifts, but this is a special day and I want you to forever remember this day. Suzie, I love you. I know it seems strange, I'm older, I have kids, I know the thoughts that have run through your mind about us being together and how we were going to make this work. We have talked about plans for next year but I wanted you to know that I am very serious about those plans. You are a special gift and I love you more each day. You have made my life an incredible adventure and I just wanted you to hold that in your heart until next year when we can seriously begin our lives together as a family. Until then, Suzie, will you marry me?"

Suzie: "What? Oh Sammie, I love you so much. Of course I will marry you."

Her answer came easily although she was choked with happy tears. He reached under the sofa and pulled out a box which he opened to reveal a very simple ring. He removed the ring from the box and slipped it on her finger, brought her hand to his lips kissing the ring on her finger. It was a perfect fit and she loved it. Her tears flowed as she stared at her hand and then looked into his eyes that were reflecting his love for her. She took his face and kissed him with a kiss straight from her soul. He gently lifted her in his arms and carried her to the bedroom that was covered in rose petals and flowers everywhere. He was such a sweetheart, how could she not love him?

Several hours later, they emerged and went to the kitchen for more surprises. He was not cooking, he had brought home a special dinner from the restaurant near his parents' house. They ate their dinner at the table filled with candles and even more flowers. Following dinner, he carried out two cupcakes with a candle in one. They fed each other the cupcakes until they were gone.

Sammie: "The cupcakes are from the boys, one from each of them."

Suzie: "Sammie, everything is just so beautiful, the flowers, the food, the cupcakes, of course the sex and my ring is beautiful. I will never forget this birthday, ever."

Sammie: "I want you to know that next year you will have a much better ring then this one. You can only wear it when you are here or we are out together for just one more year. You will have to leave it here for now and I'll show you where we can keep it."

Suzie: "I know, I don't like the idea but it's what we have to do, so it's okay."

She looked down at her finger and chills went through her, he was hers and she was his, this is perfect, everything was going to be perfect. They spent several more hours laying on the living room floor just talking. Talking about nothing really and those were the times that Suzie liked the best. She felt closer to him during those intimate moments. They held hands, kissed occasionally, but mostly they just talked.

Suzie: "Um, Sammie there is something coming up at school that I am pretty much being forced to do and I really would love it if you would come with me."

Sammie: "What's that?"

Suzie: "The senior prom."

Sammie burst out in laughter. Suzie looked at him inquisitively.

Suzie: "What's so funny?"

Sammie: "Oh Suzie, I love you so much but how in the world do you think we could pull that off?"

Suzie: "I hadn't thought of how, I just know I'm pretty much being forced to go and I don't want to. I don't want to go with anyone but you."

Sammie: "I can't do that Suzie. It's not that I wouldn't want to but it would be really hard to figure it all out and we don't want to cause any problems right now when things are going good."

Suzie: "I guess you're right. I suppose I can ask Renee's brother if he would go with me. God I don't even like that kid but I guess he will do. I'll just be glad when it's over. I'm only doing it for my mother. Things are so bad at home that she asked me about going and when I said I didn't want to, she really seemed upset. I just thought it would be a nice thing to do for her."

Sammie: "Yes it will be. I honestly don't know how we could even pull that off. I know Gary will go with Kim but that's different, her parents are okay with them. It would be nice if we had the same situation."

104

Suzie: "I know, it's getting harder and harder to be away from you. I miss having you hold me when I fall asleep, I miss making your breakfast in the morning, well some mornings, and I actually do miss the boys. I can't wait until they know what's going on. When can we tell them?"

Sammie: "I was thinking we could tell them just before we leave but we have some time before we have to figure all that out. Sam asked me if you had a brother in the school he goes to again."

Suzie: "What? That's right, they are the same age. What did you tell him?"

Sammie: "It's okay, I told him I wasn't sure and that the next time he saw you he could ask you. It bought us some time and hopefully he'll forget."

Suzie: "Wow, I guess we really do have to be careful, we don't need any problems right now."

With that said, Sammie took her in his arms and right where they were he took her to the moon and back a couple of times before she fell asleep in his arms. At some point during the night she felt him lift her off the floor and carry her to the bedroom. He laid her down, kissed her gently on the nose, told her happy birthday again and slid in beside her to sleep. She heard him whisper in her ear, "I love you so much." She fell asleep contented.

Suzie woke up the next morning to the scent of coffee permeating through the house, along with bacon frying and knew he was in the kitchen. She went to the bathroom and returned before he came into the room. She pretended to be asleep and felt him sit on the bed. Gently kissing her to wake her, she responded in kind. Their breakfast was delicious. His skills at making breakfast were amazing, unlike his dinner preparation skills.

She hated that they would have to go their own ways later today but she did not want to think about that. She looked down at her finger graced with her ring. She loved it and promised him she would never take it off. He reminded her again that she would have to leave it at the house when they weren't together and reluctantly she agreed with his reasoning. Not wanting to think about issues when they weren't together, she leaned over and kissed him gently on the lips thanking him for the wonderful breakfast. Everything else was going to have to wait for a while as they would be busy for the next couple of hours.

The entire afternoon was spent talking more about what Sammie had planned for her 18th birthday. She really wanted everyone in her small world to celebrate their wedding, but knew that would be impossible. She decided then that they could find a really nice chapel in Vegas for the ceremony and then nothing would ever matter again, except she would be his wife and she liked the sound of that.

It was getting close to the time they had to leave to pick up the boys. She tucked her ring in its special place until she could wear it again and they left. The boys were a little quiet when they arrived at his Mom's house. It surprised her that Teddy came running over to her and hugged her. She really liked that he was responsive to her and she hugged him back. Sammie's Mom walked out of the house while the boys were telling them what they had done that weekend. Sammie told her that they could not stay this time but would get together soon. His mom smiled and came to Suzie to give her a hug. Suzie liked her and it was plain that she liked Suzie. The boys got in the car and off they went back to the house.

Leaving was always hard because Suzie had to go home to 'hell'. She so hated things at the house especially now that she and Sammie had a plan but she did have some news. Kim and Gary were having an engagement party in a couple of weeks and that would be fun to attend. She only wished Sammie could go with her. Soon, she thought.

Chapter 20

The weeks went quickly and it was time for the engagement party. Jim and Carol hardly spoke to each other but they did speak to a few of the people that were there. Suzie knew everyone and had a really good time. She was so happy for Kim and wanted only the best for her. Suzie spent some time in the kitchen with Kim's cousin and was given a couple of drinks so she felt really good when it was time to go home. Several times she caught herself almost telling others about Sammie and the recent events and she had to be careful, alcohol tended to give Suzie a loose tongue. When they got home, her father told her they wanted to talk to her. They told her that after she graduated in about two months, they were going to be separating. What? This was not the conversation she was expecting. They wanted to know if she wanted to go to live with her mother in Connecticut or stay with her father. First of all, she was going to start Berkeley in the fall, her friends were here so she was going to stay here, end of story. She learned that Joe would be going to live with their mother. Suzie's decision did not sit well with her mother and she started crying. Suzie went to her room, she just didn't want to deal with this, not after a great day at Kim's party.

The following weeks were a blur. Prom came and went. Suzie went with Renee's brother and hated it. It seemed to make her mother happy and she guessed that was the best part of it. It certainly would not be a night she would want to remember. Sammie was not really happy about the whole situation, even though he took it well. He even switched his schedule to work for a couple of the guys who wanted to go to the prom and were able to.

With all of this out of the way, the only thing to look forward to was graduating high school. Suzie could not wait to finish and be out of there. She really hated that school and never felt like she fit in even though there were some nice people there. She had bittersweet feelings about that town. She hated that she had to move there but if they had not done so, she would have never met Sammie. She just wanted this over.

For those couple of months they were not able to spend much time together. Some of those interludes were spent in the downstairs room, however, Suzie always laughed about it because she knew the boys knew what they were up to. Sammie kept trying to convince her that she was wrong, however, Sam would occasionally give her that 'mad' look he had and it always made Suzie smile.

It was during one of these times in May when she noticed that Sammie was a bit quiet and she did not like the look on his face. Something was different and she wanted to know what it was.

> Suzie: "Sammie, what's bothering you? I can sense that something is not right."
>
> Sammie: "Are you still taking the birth control pills? Have you missed any of them?"
>
> Suzie: "I am absolutely taking them and no, I haven't missed any of them. Why?"
>
> Sammie: "I want you to make an appointment with the doctor tomorrow and when you go, I want to go with you. I want to make sure you are okay."
>
> Suzie: "I can do that, but why?"
>
> Sammie: "Uh, baby, I think you might be pregnant."
>
> Suzie: "What? WHAT? But how, I'm on the pill, what are you talking about?"
>
> Sammie: "Yes baby, I think you are pregnant. And how? I really don't have to explain that to you do I?"
>
> Suzie: "I had my period a couple of weeks ago, it was light and only lasted for a couple of days but it can't be. Oh dear God, what are we going to do?"
>
> Sammie: "Have you felt nauseous at all or been sick for no reason?"
>
> Suzie: "There have been a few days that I woke up nauseous but just thought it was something I ate."
>
> Sammie: "Let's see what the doctor says."
>
> Suzie: "Oh God Sammie, what are we going to do if I am?"

Sammie: "Let's not get ahead of ourselves. First the doctor and then we will figure out what to do if you are. Just remember, I do love you."

That evening before she left, Sammie was really quiet. This bothered Suzie because she was upset and when she asked if he was okay, he just kept telling her that he was tired. He had been really sweet to her after she told him about her parents separating and now he seemed so distant. She knew he did not want any more kids but what in the world were they going to do if she was pregnant. She went home with the weight of the world on her shoulders.

She made the appointment with the doctor for the next day. What the hell were they going to do? She couldn't be pregnant, not now. Oh, Dear God, please not now. She called Sammie to let him know when the appointment was and he said that was fine, he could take his lunch at that time.

The next day she left school early and went to get Sammie at work. He greeted her with a sweet kiss and even had her ring with him. He slipped it on her finger and she smiled. They drove to the doctor and he was a little chattier than he had been the last couple of days. Suzie was called into the office and Sammie went with her. Suzie changed into that cute little gown that opened in the back and they giggled about it. The doctor came in and Sammie didn't hesitate, he just told him that they needed to know if she was pregnant.

He did not want any more kids, God, he had four already. Suzie started crying and Sammie went to her to comfort her while the doctor stepped out of the room.

Suzie: "What are we going to do if I'm pregnant? You don't want any more kids, this is just not a good thing."

Sammie: "Let's see what the doctor says."

Suzie: "What would make you think I'm pregnant? If I am, what the hell are we going to do?"

Sammie: "Baby, I have four kids and there is a difference that I sense in you. Let's just calm down and see what he says. If you are, we will figure this all out. Please, baby, trust me."

Suzie: "I've been doing good with trusting you so far which has been very difficult for me but I just don't know what we are going to do."

The doctor came back in and told them that it would be too soon for him to know by exam but he could do blood and urine tests to find out, they wouldn't have the answer until tomorrow though. That was fine and they gave him Sammie's work and home numbers to call. The last thing she needed was that call going to her house. This couldn't be, it just couldn't be.

She took Sammie back to work and went home. No one was home and for that she was relieved, she went to her room. What the hell was she going to do now? She was sure that Sammie would leave her if she was pregnant, he had told her emphatically that he did not want any more kids. This was not the way things were supposed to go. She looked down and saw the ring was still on her finger. She called Sammie and told him to stop by the store on his way home so she could give him the ring back. She also knew that Jean would be there and if there was ever a time she needed to talk to her, it was then.

Suzie got ready for work and got there early so she could talk to Jean. After telling her what Sammie was thinking, she started crying. Jean calmed her down and told her that from what she saw of Sammie and how very much he loved her, it would all be okay. Suzie told her that it wouldn't be, she would have to tell her father because the baby would be born before she turned 18. She was beyond upset. Sammie showed up after work and she gave him her ring. He had asked the boss if they could talk in the stock room for a minute and the boss was fine with that because he knew something was seriously wrong.

Sammie: "Suzie, let's just see what the doctor says tomorrow. If you are pregnant we will deal with it the best way we can. The last thing I want is for you to be upset. Let's just be grateful that if you are, it happened toward the end of school for you. I also want you to know that no matter what, I will be there for you and I still do love you."

Suzie: "Oh Sammie, this is just horrible if I am. Oh my God, I can't think straight right now."

Sammie: "Remember, I do love you, we will figure it out. I need to get home to the boys, I'll call you later."

Suzie: "Sammie, I love you too. I just don't know what to feel. I'll talk to you later."

After a quick kiss he was gone. Work dragged on that night and she already knew the next day would also. She told Jean but she was not going to tell anyone else, not even Kim. Finally, the night was over and she got home as quickly as she could so she could talk to Sammie and it wasn't long before he called.

Sammie: "Hi baby."

Suzie: "Hi, I just don't know what to do, I'm so scared."

Sammie: "I know, I am too. I'm sorry I was quiet for the past couple of days but I just kind of know what the answer is going to be. Have you been sick at all today?"

Suzie: "No, not today."

Sammie: "If we need to, I will make another appointment for us to see the doctor when he calls. There will be things you will need to do. I love you Suzie, and no matter what happens I am not going to leave you so please get that thought out of your head."

Suzie: "Oh God, why now? Sammie, you told me that you didn't want any more kids. I don't even know if I want any kids. I don't even know what to do with a baby."

Sammie: "I do know that sometimes the pills don't always work as the doctor told us today. Can you get here this weekend?"

Suzie: "I will make sure I do. What about the boys, they don't need to know this right now. I'm not even going to tell Kim, but Jean knows."

Sammie: "I figured you told Jean and that's fine, you need someone to talk to but let's just keep this to ourselves for now until we figure out what we are going to do."

Suzie: "Sammie, I love you and I'm so sorry, this shouldn't have happened."

Sammie: "I love you too and we will figure it out, it's not just your fault, silly. It still takes two to make babies."

She knew that he was trying to make it easier for her by what he said but there was a serious pit in her stomach. She really didn't even pay attention when he sang to her. After they hung up, Suzie went to her room and just cried herself to sleep. She had no idea what time the doctor would call Sammie and since she was supposed to be in school, she couldn't talk to him until after. Tomorrow was going to be a long and torturous day.

Chapter 21

The day dragged on and on. Kim kept asking her if she was okay and Suzie just said she was upset about her mother taking her brother and leaving. She couldn't leave school because they were watching the seniors closely and she had to do a credit check with the guidance counselor before she left that day. What else could possibly go wrong? She only hoped that she had enough credits and all would be good for her to graduate. She couldn't even think about that right now. She found herself sitting in her last class with her hand on her stomach. Oh, God, a baby. The boys were fine, they were older, but what the hell was she going to do with a baby? She didn't even like babies that much. Kids were great, but babies not so much.

Finally, the last class was over and she went to the guidance office. She learned she had enough credits and everything was fine for her to graduate. Then she was handed a note, Sammie had called the school and left a message for her to go to his house right after school. She left school which was the last thing on her mind anyway.

When she arrived at Sammie's he was pacing in the driveway. He got in her car and told her to drive to the doctor's office. Then he told her the test had come back positive. Before they discussed anything, they needed to see the doctor. She had started crying and pulled over to let Sammie drive, she couldn't see. After he had told her the results, he had gotten very quiet and this only upset Suzie more. They waited to be called in to see the doctor with a canyon of silence between them. Suzie just sat there stunned.

Finally, they were called in. The doctor told them that the baby would be born right around Christmas. He gave her a prescription for vitamins and told her that if she had any morning sickness to eat crackers and drink ginger ale. Oh my God, what were they going to do?

After making an appointment for the following month, they got back in the car and left with Sammie driving again and he took them to the back side of the lake. That lake, she really hated that lake and right now she just wanted this to be a huge nightmare. They arrived at the lake and he shut the car off.

Sammie: "This is not exactly what we had planned. I know I told you I didn't want any more kids but I always knew this was a possibility, we are going to figure this out and we will make it work. I still love you and can't imagine my life without you. Having a baby will just serve to connect us together on a much deeper level."

Suzie: "I just don't know how this is going to work. I don't turn 18 until next March and that's three months after the baby comes. I don't even know what to do with a baby. Yeah, I've babysat but this will be a little different and what about us?"

Sammie: "I know, it's going to be tough but we are going to get through this and be fine. The most important thing is that we do this together. I don't want you to tell anyone, not even Kim. I know Jean already knows and that's fine, you do need someone besides me, but promise you won't tell anyone else right now because we can't risk your father finding out until we are ready to tell him."

Suzie: "I promise. What about the boys, what are they going to think? They already have a sister and a younger brother, they just might not like this too much."

Sammie: "Don't worry about the boys, they will be fine. Let's just give us some time to think this through and come up with a plan. We are going to be a family and it's all going to be okay, I promise."

Suzie: "How could this happen? I took the pills every day."

Sammie: "Do I really have to tell you how this happened? The doctor explained it and it's done. We are going to be fine. I just wish you could be with me now, I want to take care of you."

They looked at each other and laughed, what else could they do. Somehow they would figure this whole mess out. Suzie's mother was going to be leaving soon and that would just leave her father to deal with, he was a little easier to deal with than her mother so that was one good thing. And to think, Suzie was going to graduate with a little someone else. Oh shit.

Sammie took her to A&W to get something to eat. He also bought some food for the boys. The boys were happy to see her, they always were. They ate in relative silence and Suzie really suspected the boys knew something was wrong because after they ate they went right to their rooms. This gave Sammie and Suzie some more private time to talk. They decided that they would just get through the next couple of months before she started showing and then they would confront her father together. What could he do? That thought made Suzie cringe.

The next couple of weeks were hard. Suzie had started having more and more bouts of morning sickness but so far had been able to hide it. She kept crackers and ginger ale hidden in her room. It helped but at night she would often think of why this had to happen now of all times. Sammie was different also, he was still attentive and caring, but his moods seemed to fluctuate quickly and was often quiet. They managed to share some special times but Suzie did not like the changes she saw in him. Whenever she confronted him about it, he assured her that everything was fine and he was just wanting her to be with him all the time so he could care for her. Things were changing and she wasn't sure what to do about it or even if there was anything she could do. She was extremely frustrated and waiting for the end of school was proving to be a challenge.

During their conversation the previous night, Sammie asked if she could get away for a couple of days after graduation. She told him she didn't know what her mother's plans were and how things were going to play out after she left. He said he understood but they needed some time alone together to really talk and not just an hour or two. More pressure, this was not her idea of what her teenage years were supposed to be. She told him she would see what she could do.

Suzie found out later that day that her father had taken a job a bit south and after her graduation he would be heading down there and staying at least two weeks. Bingo, she could make some plans to be with Sammie, they seriously needed this time together. Graduation would be on a Saturday and her mother was planning on leaving that Monday so she made arrangements to have that following weekend off from work. This way Sammie would not have to take off any more work. He had already taken off for the two previous doctor's appointments and would leave work to be with Suzie when he knew she was really upset.

Chapter 22

Graduation day finally arrived. Suzie was suffering from a major bout of morning sickness and just wanted this to be all over. She sat alone in her room quietly nibbling on crackers and sipping ginger ale. Sammie had supplied her with more and she had a corner in her closet where she hid her stash. With time moving quickly, her grandparents and other guests arrived. She loved being around her extended family but this time it was just not the same. They knew she knew that her mother was leaving and it just made things pretty difficult. Suzie had to leave early to meet Kim at the school to get ready. On the way she said, "Okay little one, let's get this over with so daddy and I can figure out just what the hell we are going to do with you."

Arriving at the school, Kim asked if Suzie was feeling okay, she told her she looked pale and not really well. Suzie told Kim she was fine, it was all just too much since she knew her mother was leaving and taking her brother with her. She so wanted to share her news with Kim, after all she was her best friend but they had agreed to keep it to themselves, at least for now. To change the subject, Suzie asked if they had made any more wedding plans. Kim told her that her mother was coming up with all kinds of things. Suzie laughed and said this is going to be exciting. Kim agreed and for just a few short moments, Suzie was able to get her mind off of the baby.

The ceremony was long, of course when school administrators give speeches, they take forever. Suzie kept finding herself with her hand resting against her stomach which she was going to have to make a conscious effort to stop. They certainly did not need anyone figuring this out. Her mind drifted and started wondering if they would have a son or a daughter. They hadn't even discussed what they hoped it would be. Then she wondered if they would even have that conversation or would they even survive all of this. Surely, he would be able to handle this better than she since she was so young and he was a pro at this stuff. Oh, God. Finally it was time for diplomas.

After the ceremony they gathered for pictures and were going back to Suzie's house for some celebrating. She didn't feel much like it but managed to put on a smile and enjoy visiting her grandparents. At least for that afternoon she was able to just set aside everything and be a 'kid' again.

Sammie called later that evening and he seemed in a better mood. She told him that this weekend they could be together and possibly more depending on when her mother left. He seemed happy about that. She asked if he was okay and he told her that he had talked to his mother. Oh, shit, then she knew. He told her yes and to not worry, they would discuss everything this coming weekend. After singing "Goodnight Sweetheart" to her they hung up and Suzie felt a bit better. She was now a high school graduate and pregnant. Great!

At work the next day, Jean was very supportive and told her that if she needed to talk or needed a place to stay because of how her father would react, she could stay with her. This made Suzie feel better about things but it should be Sammie that she stayed with. Jean agreed but also told her that she was afraid that there would be a huge fight with her father. She was able to get off work at two that day and drove home. She had to keep a low profile with Sammie because she wasn't sure what was going on at home. When she arrived, no one was home. There was a note on her bed that told her that her mother had taken her brother to 'visit' her grandmother in Connecticut. On the kitchen counter was another note with $100 from her father saying he was going to be gone for about two weeks and if she needed anything he left her a phone number. Well great, two days after graduating high school, 17 years old and she was alone. Well not quite, she did have a little one with her.

Suzie wandered around the house. It just seemed too quiet. All of a sudden she ran to the bathroom. This morning sickness was supposed to be in the morning, why was she having bouts of it throughout the day? They had another doctor's appointment in a couple of weeks and she would have to remember to ask. It seemed eerie at home so she went downstairs to the piano. She did not play much anymore, but she sat there that day and played her heart out. She figured that in the next few days this was going to be gone. Was this better or was it better when they were all at home. Even the fighting was better than this empty feeling. Who was going to help her through all this baby stuff? Frustration just caused her to play louder and louder. Finally, the tears came. She just wondered why they even had to leave Petersville in the first place, none of this mess would have happened had they stayed. Nothing offered at this school to keep her interested, being raped, being pregnant. This was just not fair.

She finished playing, fed the dog and went to Sammie's. She had the key and she knew the boys would be there but that was okay, they were a good diversion right now. The boys had opened the garage door when they saw she was there, she drove into the garage and they came running out to greet her. They closed the garage door and Teddy took her hand as they went upstairs. They asked if she was going to stay the night. Suzie just laughed because she knew and had been telling Sammie that they knew more than they were letting on, now she knew this to be true. They were all excited to tell her that they were going to their Nana's this weekend for about a week. They liked being with their grandmother. Good, they would have the weekend to themselves. They needed it because they had not had much time alone since finding out she was pregnant.

They heard the front door open and told her they were going down the street. Suzie suspected this was planned but was grateful that Sammie had thought ahead enough to have them gone at least for a little while. The boys ran down the stairs as Sammie was coming up the stairs and there was a fit of giggles from all of them. Suzie sat back on the sofa and just closed her eyes. Those laughing moments were good, she liked to hear them all laugh.

She opened her eyes as she felt Sammie sit in front of her on the coffee table. That damn table, she knew this was going to be serious. He leaned forward and kissed her gently as he placed a hand on her stomach. She asked how his day had been and he said it had been revolving. That was a joke they shared since Sammie worked at a local tire store.

> Sammie: "You've been crying. Suzie, please, I wish you would stop getting so upset. It isn't good for you or the baby. We are going to figure this out together and we are going to make this work. Yes, we should have had more time and shouldn't have to be making these kind of plans right now but this is what we have to do. We will figure this out because I love you more than anything in this world."

> Suzie: "Sammie I love you too, it's just that all of this has been so overwhelming. Graduation, my mother leaving, the baby, you have been acting very distant and I'm just scared that you are going to leave me to deal with this mess myself. I don't know what to do, remember I'm only 17 years old, I don't know which way to turn right now."

> Sammie: "I know baby, but I am here for you. I had a long talk with my mother the other night. She adores you, the boys adore you, she will do whatever she can to help us, and I want us to be a family and we will be. Mom said she would be there if you ever feel like you need her. She is excited for us and for her too. She did say to not tell the boys until after we tell your father which we will do just before you really start showing. It's all going to be good. Mom suggested that we invite your father here and have her here with us also, she has this magical way of keeping everyone calm. Then we can tell him. Yes, he will probably raise hell but what can he do, nothing."

> Suzie: "You make it sound so easy. I'll probably get thrown out of the house, what am I going to do then?"

> Sammie: "You think too much, but what's the matter with this house? I know we talked about selling it after we got married and we can still do that, you deserve a home of your own and you will have it. If that all happens then there is plenty of room for you here silly. It's all going to work."

> Suzie: "I haven't been able to think much about anything lately. It's all just too much to take in at once. I am glad I have you and I do love you."

This conversation made Suzie feel a little better but then she had to run to the bathroom. This time Sammie was right behind her, rubbing her back and applying a cold compress to her forehead. He didn't even think twice about being

120

right there with her while she got sick. He gave her a glass of water to rinse her mouth with and then scooped her up and carried her to the sofa. Leaving her there he went to the kitchen and brought back a plate of crackers and a glass of ginger ale. He shared that he had also stocked up on supplies there which caused Suzie to smile. Maybe, just maybe things would be as he said and it would all work out. If only she knew.

She started to doze off, then heard the boys coming in but kept her eyes closed. She heard them ask their father if she was okay. Sammie told them she was just tired after the busy weekend she had and to be quiet and help him in the kitchen. "Oh Lord, another holy mess" she thought. She did manage to doze off for a while and woke when Sammie sat on the sofa and gently kissed her awake. Her eyes fluttered open. He told her that he had fed the boys, they were in their rooms and had promised to be quiet so she could rest and she smiled. He then brought out a tray of food. Oh, God, food, she ran for the bathroom with him right on her heels.

After getting sick this time she felt a lot better. He sat next to her on the sofa and took her hand. He slipped her ring on her finger and she smiled. She picked at the food and he told her that she had to eat more than that, he fed her. Thankfully he had not made anything too spicy or acidic. He cleaned up the mess and came back to the sofa so they could talk. They were excited about spending the weekend together. She told him that she had to work until two on Friday but then did not have to be back until Monday. This was going to be a grand weekend. She did have to work the next day but she wanted to keep her ring this time. He let her since he knew that her father was out of town and that she needed to feel the connection the ring offered her.

Saying goodbye was getting more and more difficult especially now that Suzie was pregnant. He was worried about her when she wasn't around because of her getting sick and not eating. She just wanted to be with him where she felt safe and loved. Keeping her ring was soothing to her that night.

Leaving Sammie's house was a little strange. It had been sunny and calm at his house but when she drove out of his neighborhood, she noticed that everything looked torn up. She drove into town, there were power lines down, and a car was' upside down so she stopped to ask someone what had happened. They told her that a tornado had gone through town. What? She turned around and headed for home, the dog was there alone and she was worried. The house was fine but the huge tree in the back was on its side, the roots had been ripped from the ground. There was a boat in the trees up the road and a pool in some other trees. Thankfully the house was fine but there was no power, however, there was phone service. She called her father to tell him what had happened and he said he was coming up but couldn't stay if everything was okay. He had to work the next day.

Sammie had made her promise him that she would call him when she got home. She did and told him what had happened in town, he said he had heard it on the news. He was frantic to know if she was okay and now that he knew she was, he could rest. While they were talking she got sick again. Returning to the phone she asked him why they called it morning sickness when she was getting sick all the time. He just laughed and said that's the way it was sometimes. She wanted to go to bed, tomorrow was an early work day. He sang "Goodnight Sweetheart" to her and they hung up.

Her father arrived and checked everything out. Assured that all was oaky and after talking together for a few minutes he had to return so he could go to work the next day. He wanted her to go to a friend's house but she had to work the next day herself. Reluctantly he said okay and if she needed anything to go to the neighbors. He left her some more money and was gone. So, this is what it was going to be like.

She laid in bed that night with her hand on her stomach, feeling better about everything and started talking to the baby. "Oh, if only you had waited to make your appearance. But you know what? Your daddy said he was going to make sure that everything would work out. Your grandmother already knows about you and she will help us." She drifted off to sleep.

Chapter 23

Suzie woke up prior to the alarm going off and ran to the bathroom. She so hated getting sick and wished this would stop, she certainly did not want anyone figuring this out. She wanted to call in sick that day but felt it better that she didn't, so she ate some crackers, drank some ginger ale and felt better. She took her vitamin and was getting ready for work when the phone rang. It was her father wanting to know if she was okay. She told him she was and that she was getting ready for work. The power was still not on but at work she could use the registers without power, he wanted her to call him later and she said she would.

She had to take several detours getting to work, they were still cleaning up the town and what a mess it was. One of the stores up from the drug store had a window blown out, glass was everywhere as well as debris littering the street. When she arrived at the store, the bosses were already there. Nothing had happened to the store but they were without power. After a quick lesson on how to use the registers manually, they opened the doors.

It was crazy busy that day and Suzie stayed until three in the afternoon. When she left she noticed they had made a lot of progress cleaning up the town, but on the way home she noticed more damage. Trees were down everywhere, a house under construction was ripped from the foundation, and the boat and pool were still in the trees. As she drove down the road, she saw a U-Haul truck, her grandfather's car and her mother's car at the house. She went in and saw that her mother had basically cleaned out the house which upset her tremendously and she ran from the house without talking to anyone and left. She went to Sammie's job, he was having a very quiet day and was able to talk with her. He told her to just pack up some stuff and go to his house. She couldn't, she would have to call her father and let him know what her mother had done. Suzie was so upset and since there was only an hour left to Sammie's day, he left early. She followed him to his house, this time not even bothering to park in the garage because she wasn't going to be able to stay too long. She ran from the car, he tried to catch her to carry her but she flew up the stairs to the bathroom. When she came out Sammie was standing in the living room with an arm around each of the boys.

> Sammie: "They are worried about you and wanted to make sure you are okay."
>
> Suzie: "I'm fine, I think just the stress of all this mess just made my stomach upset."

If only they knew, and she wondered what they would think as they ran off to their rooms. Was she really ready to take them on? Yes, she was, they were great boys and she was starting to love them. Sammie took her hand and lead her to the sofa where they sat and discussed what she had found at her house and she started crying. This was just not the way it was supposed to be. He understood, after all it had not been that long ago when his family was ripped apart. Damn divorce, why do people even get married if they don't love each other. Suzie vowed right there that no matter what, she would make sure that her family stayed together forever, and if things were that bad then they would just have to make it work until at least the kids were grown. She didn't know if this mess was easier for her at this age or on Sammie's kids at their age. They certainly shouldn't have to go through things like this, they were innocent and it just wasn't fair that they could not see their sister or brother and it wasn't going to be fair that she couldn't see Joe.

After discussing this with Sammie, he assured her that it was difficult but kids do bounce back and yes it was terribly unfair to his kids to be separated and he hated it. He then told her that he was going to have the boys again for the entire summer, his ex-wife was not going to swap the kids around this year. So, now Suzie knew why he had been so upset and she should have figured that out earlier. This made her feel bad because it had been quite a while since he saw the other two kids. It also upset her that she wouldn't be able to meet them and really wanted to. It just didn't seem fair and she asked why he didn't go see them. He told her that his ex-wife wouldn't let him see them which caused Suzie to not have good thoughts about his ex-wife but kept those thoughts to herself.

The conversation turned toward the coming weekend, she could be there Friday in time to take the boys to his mother's. Sammie was really happy about that because he told her that his mother wanted to talk to her which made her wonder if this was going to be good or bad. He assured her it was good. He leaned in to give her a kiss and she ran to the bathroom with him on her heels again. This was pretty bad, it was nothing but dry heaves. Suzie hated to be sick to her stomach and this was just getting to be a bit much. Sammie carried her to the sofa where she found a plate of crackers and a glass of ginger ale waiting. She looked up toward the kitchen and saw the boys standing there with sheepish grins on their cute faces. She smiled and they told her that they wanted her to feel better and that's what Nana gave them when they were sick. How sweet she thought, smiling at them as she ate a cracker.

Sammie was getting concerned about how often she was getting sick and everything that was going on at her house, although he did not say anything to her but would certainly ask the doctor the next time they saw him. He did not feel like cooking so he told Sam to come with him to go and get a pizza asking if she thought she could eat it. She said no and that she was going to have to go home anyway. She loved pizza and that told him that she was really not feeling well so he did not push the issue. He made her promise to call him after she spoke with her father. She handed him back her ring on the sly and he carried her down the stairs to the car. They told each other how much they loved each other, shared a quick kiss and with that she was gone.

When she walked into the house and saw what was missing her heart sank, she ran to her room, that was intact but her mother had taken just about everything. How in the world can parents do this to their kids and she wondered what was going through her brother's head because all he knew was that they were supposed to be visiting their grandmother for a few days. He idolized their father. Suzie made the call to her father to tell him what she found, he told her that he would be there in about an hour. She then called Sammie and he knew right away that she was upset but there was nothing they could do because her father would be there soon. Suzie wasn't sure if he was staying there that night or not so she couldn't plan anything. They hung up just before her father walked in the door.

His reaction was as expected, he was furious. Her mother had left two plates, two forks, a pot and pan, two towels, and he started ranting about what was he supposed to do? She let him rant. He made a phone call using her trick of going out on the back deck to talk so she couldn't hear him. When her father got off the phone, he called her to the living room. This was when he told her that they would do some shopping to replace some things. He also told her that he was going to be working down south for quite a while and would only be able to get there occasionally. If she wasn't home when he got there he would make sure to leave her some money for anything she might need. This was just not fair and all she wanted was to be with Sammie. She asked about this weekend and he told her he was going to have to work the whole weekend. Apparently it was a big job for IBM and it would keep him busy most of the time. They went out to dinner and even though she did not want to eat because she did not feel well, she had to, so she did.

While eating her father asked about the time she was spending with Sammie. What? How did he know? He said he just knew that was all. He told her that he did not want her getting too serious with him because he was just plain too old for her. She kept her cool assuring him that she was going to be busy with work, getting ready for Berkeley and helping Kim with wedding plans to see much of him, if at all. That seemed to appease him or at least that's what she thought. He then told her that she could come and go as she pleased with no questions but just keep in mind that he's too old for you. They went home and he left again.

It was kind of late, but she needed to talk to Sammie so she called him. Thankfully he was still up and was glad she had called. He had been very worried about her and was starting to get irritated that they had to stay apart, especially now. She told him about the conversation with her father which upset Sammie. Not because he had told her to stay away from him but because he seemed to be basically abandoning her and she couldn't be with him all the time. She was pretty much on

128

her own which was good for them, but he held quiet suspicion that her father was having her followed which he did not tell her. They were going to have to be really careful for a while. He told her he would see her tomorrow afternoon, that he loved her to the moon and then sang "Goodnight Sweetheart" to her. She just loved when he did that.

Chapter 24

The next day couldn't go fast enough and after work Suzie went to Sammie's. She already had a bag in the trunk where it would stay until they returned from his mother's. The boys were playing around, she could hear them outside. The garage door opened and Sam greeted her with his winning smile, a smile that she did not see all that often and it bothered her because it looked good on him. Teddy was more outgoing and when Suzie was around he was right by her side as often as he could be and today was no different. Teddy jumped in the car for the ride into the garage which Suzie thought was cute. Teddy loved her Mustang and liked to ride in it, she vowed to take them on more outings in the Mustang. She would have to talk to Sammie about this.

The kids led her upstairs, they had made a valiant effort to clean the house and had done a great job especially in their rooms. Their bags were also packed for their week with nana which had them excited. They took her by the hand to the sofa where she found a plate of crackers and a glass of ginger ale. Sam told her that Teddy had insisted they do that because they wanted her to feel good. That was one of the most precious things they had ever done for her and it made her love them even more. They sat on the sofa with her, one on each side and talked. They talked so much she had to hush one at a time and this was something different from the way Sam was normally. She wondered what had inspired this difference but wasn't going to question it, she was just enjoying the conversation. Even though she was not feeling ill, she ate a couple of the crackers and drank some ginger ale. They asked if she wanted more, she told them she was fine.

They heard him before she did and their excitement heightened, they wanted to get to Nana's. She heard Sammie open the door and jokingly call out, "Who's in my house?" This caused fits of laughter as he bounded up the stairs carrying a fistful of roses. The boys ran to their rooms, Sammie walked to her and got down on his knees. He handed her the flowers, kissed her lips sweetly and told her that they were for the greatest and most beautiful woman in his life. Suzie smiled and just simply kissed him back. With everything that had gone on in her life since moving to Martin's Cove, he was the one constant person she could truly count on. She loved him with her entire being, had come to trust him, only him, and could never imagine life without him.

On the way to his Mom's house, Suzie told Sammie to stop the car now, she jumped from the car and got sick. God, was this ever going to stop. Sammie came to her side and just rubbed her back, he was getting seriously concerned at how often she was sick because it was obvious that she was losing weight, but did not say anything. He helped her back to the car and Teddy, oh so cute Teddy, handed her some crackers telling her he brought them with him in case she needed them. She smiled and slowly ate the crackers which helped and by the time they got to his Mom's house, she felt better.

Sammie's Mom was in the driveway when they arrived and she went right to Suzie to give her a hug. She told her how good it was to see her but she looked pale, she did not mention her weight loss. Suzie told her about getting sick so much and his mother assured her that it happened sometimes but she should be feeling better soon. She reiterated the same things Sammie had told her about being there to help if she was needed and how excited she was which warmed Suzie's heart as she turned to see Sammie leaning on the car smiling. The boys had run off somewhere and Sammie told his mom that they were going to go and have a nice dinner. They would be back to get the boys the following Sunday. That was fine with his mom and they left. His mom was doing her part to help with their relationship because she seriously wanted Suzie to stay in her son's life.

Sammie took her to the restaurant close to his mother's house that she liked because it was elegant and the food was very good. It was also romantic and right then Suzie could use a good dose of that which Sammie knew. He had become so good at anticipating her every need, desire, could read her moods and they had gotten to the point of being able to finish each other's sentences. This had to be love, it just had to be. She still loved the way she felt when she was with him, as if nothing else in the world mattered especially the times they went out publicly. Dinner was exquisite, Suzie was famished, and she ate everything that was served to her, picking a few pieces from Sammie's plate also. He just smiled and asked if she wanted another order which caused her to laugh and she said no, she was going to get fat enough.

They wanted that night to be just about the two of them, Suzie was in a playful mood so she went to the drawer that held her sweet nighties. She found a gift which she opened and found a red outfit that was even tinier than the black one. She giggled uncontrollably because this would not work when she had a huge belly, she changed into that tiny outfit. Entering the living room she saw the candles and heard the music. "In the Still of the Night" emanated from the stereo. She walked to Sammie who just stood there watching her smiling and took him in her arms as he told her that she looked amazing. They danced slowly around the room, she took his face in her hands, told him how very much she loved him, could never imagine any other place in the world she would rather be then or forever. She kissed his lips, he responded but she already knew what he was feeling. He carried her into the bedroom and they stayed there the entire night, finally falling asleep entwined together as was their habit, absolute perfection.

The next morning they fixed breakfast together but all Suzie wanted was some toast, her stomach was upset again.

Suzie: "This baby is giving me fits. If this is any indication of what we are in for, God help us."

Sammie: "Then it must take after me because you are just too sweet to give anyone fits."

He actually seemed to be getting excited about the baby, or so it seemed which made Suzie feel good because she was still having serious doubts about what to do with it. They cleaned up the kitchen together, went to sit in the living room when Sammie took her face in his hands and asked if she wanted to try something different, something they had never done before. Now what in the world could that be, she really thought from everything she had learned this last year that they had pretty much covered all these bases. Well, to her shock and as she would find out that was not true, he asked if she had ever watched a porno movie? What? When would she have done that? She has only been with him, but she had heard of them and knew what they were. The first thought that came to mind was what her grandmother had said, be a lady on his arm and a whore in his bed. Well, okay, this would be different and sure, why not.

He took her to the bedroom, took out a movie projector and set it so that it would broadcast on the headboard. This was pretty exciting. The movie came on, he slid up the bed next to her and had his arm around her. As they watched, Suzie concluded that this was pretty cool but what they were doing was everything he had already done to her or so she thought. He whispered in her ear asking if she would be willing to do what they were doing in the movie, she thought sure why not and told him so. It was then that she realized the woman in the movie was tied to the bed. Oh my. Wait one minute here.

Suzie: "You want to tie me to the bed? You will let me go won't you?"

Sammie laughed and laughed.

Sammie: "Of course I'll let you go. When we play around like this its fine as long as we have complete trust in each other. I trust you with my life and I think you feel the same way."

Suzie: "I do trust you with my life and if you want to play like that, sure, I'm willing to try it."

They proceeded to copy the movie and Suzie thought she had been to the moon previously, well this time she went to Mars. This man certainly knew what he was doing with her and she had to admit that she really liked the things he was teaching her. She asked him if he had any more of those movies and he said he did but not now, one at a time, we don't want to get bored with this type of play. Then he assured her that this was not going to happen all the time, just once in a while to make things different. Good, she was worried that he was getting bored with her. Oh, not the case.

They did not feel like sitting around the house all afternoon so they decided to just take a ride to wherever. After getting sick again they got ready to go and left, heading north. Just driving around was fun, especially with Sammie because she never knew what to expect. They drove to a little park about an hour north of town, different from the park they had previously visited and it was beautiful. The sun was shining which made it a beautiful and warm day. There were picnic tables there, he chose one and they sat down to talk.

Sammie: "I wanted to talk to you away from the house, the kids, your father and everything, just you and I. Suzie, I love you so much. This whole thing has been quite a shock for me as well as you. I know this is hard, it's hard on me too not being able to be with you all the time especially knowing you are getting so sick. It took a bit for me to digest the thought of having another child. I know I told you I didn't want any more kids, but my wedding gift to you was going to be telling you I wanted a child with you. I can only imagine what this baby will look like. A little girl who looks just like you or a little boy with a combination of us, it doesn't matter at all as long as it's healthy and I will do everything in my power to make sure he/she is happy as well as his/her mother."

Suzie: "Oh Sammie, I was so worried that you really didn't want to have this baby. I wasn't ready for this to happen now and actually I never gave having a child a thought. You already have Sam, Cara, Teddy and Jack. You really don't need another one but I'm glad you are happy about it. Maybe now I can start being happy about it."

Sammie: "Oh baby, I want you to be happy, this is our child. Yes, the timing is off but who says it's ever perfect to have a child. We are going to make this work and we are going to promise each other that we will always put each other first."

Suzie: "Of course because I want all the kids to be happy. I know it's hard for Sam and Teddy to be away from the other kids and I wish we could do something about that. Maybe in time, we can get Cara and Jack here and have all the kids together at least for a little bit of time."

Sammie: "We will have to see about that. They were supposed to be switched again this year but it's not going to happen and it's been two years since I've seen the other two. I call them every week but it just isn't the same. Promise me that if we do not last together that you won't move away and take this baby with you. Please promise me that."

Suzie: "I promise. I'm not going anywhere, we are going to have a baby to raise. I don't care if it is a boy or a girl, I just want it to look like you. I love your hair, your eyes, your nose, your mouth, oh heck, I love you."

Sammie: "I love you too. Mom is so excited. She knows she really can't react right now because we don't want anyone to know. You weren't upset that I talked to her, are you?"

Suzie: "No, you know I talked to Jean so why would I be upset, you need to talk to someone too. I was just upset by your initial reaction and I thought you were going to leave me."

Sammie: "I'm sorry baby, I was upset because I really didn't want any more kids, but now that I've gotten used to the idea, I'm kind of liking it a lot. It will be fun to have a child with you and you are going to make a good mother and be a positive influence on the boys. They already adore you."

Suzie: "I have grown to love those two. I really want to start doing some things with them. I know I have to take it slowly but I would love to take them for lunch and take them places, just the three of us."

Sammie: "Oh, I see how this is going to be, just the three of you while dear old dad is toiling away at work."

Suzie: "Yup, we can also do things together as a family as time goes on. First they are going to have to get used to the idea of me being around more."

Sammie: "Yes and I want to take all this slowly. After we tell your father, we can tell them about the baby. I'm really hoping that since the baby will be born in December that we will be able to get married before."

Suzie: "Oh what a horrible thought, I'll be so fat."

Sammie: "I wasn't married to Sam's mom when he was born, I adopted him after and I don't want that for our child. I want us together before it's born."

Suzie: "Well that sounds good to me too. Do you really think this will work?"

Sammie: "It's going to be tough, especially with your father, but we will make it work because we want it to and I love you."

They sat and watched the sun reflecting off of the lake. Sammie had his arm around Suzie and pulled her close, he cherished the times they could spend together like this and he knew she did too. It was getting late and they were hungry, so they left the park and went to the restaurant tucked in the woods that they had seen on the way to the park. It was a rustic, quiet, gorgeous little log cabin with creaky floors and a huge fireplace. Their lunch was amazing and they both ate heartily.

Suzie: "Where did you learn to cook?"

Sammie: "Why?"

Suzie: "Well your breakfasts are good but some of your dinners leave a lot to be desired."

Sammie: "I really didn't know how to cook. Do you think you can do a better job?"

Suzie: "I sure can. I'll tell you what, when I figure out what my schedule is next week and what my father will be doing, I'll cook a meal one night."

Sammie: "You're on."

They drove home talking more about the baby as Suzie found herself more and more resting her hand on her stomach. She had to make a conscious effort to watch that because someone was bound to figure it out if she continued to do it. They arrived home just after dark and the house was eerily silent. He went in and turned on a light and then came out to carry her upstairs. She loved the attention he showered on her, how he always seemed to make her feel special. Even though some thought this was all so wrong, it was just so right.

Chapter 25

When they got up the stairs, there were two presents sitting on the coffee table. He handed her the smaller one first. She looked at him and decided that she really had to start reciprocating these little gifts for him. She opened it not knowing what to expect and inside were two tiny tee shirts. One was pink and had 'Daddy's Girl' written on it, the other was blue and had 'Mommy's Boy' on it. Suzie burst into tears, they were adorable and so tiny, what was she going to do with this little critter? She hugged him so hard and kissed him. This was the first time she felt any real excitement about the baby at all. He really was going to make a great daddy to their baby, he was already a great daddy to the boys.

The other one was a larger box, she had learned to love it when he spoiled her. She opened it and found another negligee inside, this one was a silky ivory. It was long, flowing and absolutely beautiful. Without saying another word, she went to the bedroom to change. When she came out she found him leaning over the stereo and already had candles lit in the room. God, would it always be this good even after they got married then she wondered what things would be like when she got fat. Shaking her head she put those thoughts out of her mind as he turned around and just stood there staring at her.

Sammie: "You look like an angel. Suzie I love you more than you can ever know. I can't imagine one second without you."

Suzie: "I can't either. Sammie, I love you with all of my heart and soul. I don't want to be any place else except right here with you."

Sammie: "And I don't want you anywhere else except right here where you belong."

The rest of the night was amazing. They were perfection together and they knew it. Whoever had doubts about them were wrong, this was going to work. They fell asleep securely tangled in each other's arms and with smiles on their faces. Suzie was certainly allowing herself to trust Sammie. She had never in her life felt as safe as she did when she was with him. Being raped seemed like a lifetime ago.

The next day dawned and this time Suzie was up making them breakfast. She had had another bout of nausea, decided to just stay up and fix breakfast for him. She made French toast and sausage, he did have what she needed to prepare that. On the way to carrying the tray into the bedroom, she felt the nausea start again. Setting the tray on the floor, she just made it to the bathroom and felt his hand on her back. She was glad he had not tripped over the tray. After this episode of getting sick, the last thing she wanted to do was eat anything so she fed him and sipped from the cup of tea he had made for her.

They talked about the doctor's appointment she had later in the week and he wanted to go with her as always and she told him it was on Wednesday at 11am. He was going to make a point of asking the doctor about her getting so sick and her weight loss. She knew that he was concerned even though he didn't say anything about it, he didn't have to. The phone rang, it was Sammie's mom telling him the boys could stay there for the next week. She wanted them to pick them up the following Sunday and plan on having dinner with them. That sounded good but Suzie was going to have to do some schedule switching for that day which was fine.

The rest of the afternoon was lazy. Suzie was going to spend that night but she had to go home to get some clothes for work the next morning. Sammie wanted to come with her and did. She went in the back way so she could see her father's truck if he was there. Luckily he wasn't. They went inside and Sammie sadly looked around at the almost empty house and he knew that Suzie was sad about that. He followed her to her room, it was the first time he had been there and he smiled when he saw how much she had crammed in that room.

Sammie: "You have enough clothes to last a year and not wear the same thing twice."

Suzie: "No I don't. Besides pretty soon I'm going to need huge clothes."

Sammie: "I know, but don't worry, we'll take care of it."

Suzie: "Could you please get my loafers from the closet?"

Sammie: "Well, okay, which ones, there are like ten pairs of them."

They laughed and she wondered how anyone could have enough clothes, that just did not make any sense. Besides his closet was just as packed, she wondered how they would fit everything in one closet, they would figure it out. She fed the dog, checked around the house and found her father's note. Oh shit, he must have come home. There was more money in the note and he had written, "I know where you are and we will talk when I get home in two weeks. I won't be back for two weeks but call me when you get home." She called her father and assured him that everything was fine, she had been out with friends and shopping with Kim, but she knew that he didn't believe her and that was the end of the conversation. Now, she had more to worry about.

Sammie read the note while she was on the phone and it angered him. He really felt his suspicious were correct and her father was either checking up on her or having her followed. This was going to be more difficult than either he or Suzie figured on.

Driving back to Sammie's she was a little testy since she was concerned about what her father was thinking. He could really cause some problems for them and she did not want that to happen, especially now. They would just have to wait until he got home to find out what this was all about. Although Suzie really wanted to cook, Sammie said they would get pizza. She wasn't sure her stomach could handle that but she would try. They went to the store to get more ginger ale and crackers when Suzie caught him in the baby aisle looking at all the stuff. She called him and said she wasn't quite ready to do that yet, she would be soon. All she could think about was her father and what he had said.

When they got back to Sammie's he opened the garage door so she could pull her car inside. He ran the pizza and groceries upstairs and came back to get her. While he was upstairs she had slipped out of the garage to the side of the house to get sick again. He came running to her to make sure she was alright. She couldn't wait to see the doctor and see if there was something else she could do for this besides the crackers and ginger ale.

When they got upstairs, he wanted her to try to eat but Suzie did not want to. Sammie was getting a little insistent, telling her that the baby needed food and wouldn't do well if she didn't eat. Her hormones must have kicked in because she started yelling at him that she did not want to eat. She started crying and Sammie was getting madder by the second. She stormed into the kitchen to get a piece of pizza and he followed her yelling at her. She threw the plate at him and that started it. They were yelling and screaming at each other and not only did Suzie throw things, he did also.

Of course, the neighbor heard them and called the police and the same sergeant appeared who came last year. They were still hot tempered when he arrived. She saw him and told him to please leave, that they were done. The sergeant told her to go outside. She never did find out what he said to Sammie and it was probably better that she didn't. The sergeant came outside to find her sitting on the planter waiting. He wanted to know what she was doing there and she told him that it was really none of his business. He then told her that if they were called to the house any more, they were going to arrest him. Again, she pleaded that they could not do that because he had two kids who had nowhere else to go. The sergeant told her they simply had to stop fighting like that. Again the sergeant asked her if her father knew she was there, she told him he knew. He told her they were going to talk to her father about this situation because of her age and she told him that she would really appreciate it if he just didn't say anything. He told her he wouldn't as long as they did not fight like this any longer, the next time they would take action. This whole time Suzie had to seriously control the urge to be sick and after, she held on to the side of the house enduring a serious bout of dry heaves. She figured out pretty quickly that the sergeant was the one who was telling her father where she was.

By the time Suzie got back inside, Sammie had cleaned up the house and was sitting on the sofa. She started crying again and just sat down on the stairs. Why did they have to fight like that? This time it was her fault because of the damn hormones and thinking this whole pregnancy thing is just not fun. She got up from the stair, walked over to the sofa, and noticed that Sammie had been crying too. He took one look at her, knew she had been sick again and just held her.

Suzie: "I'm so sorry. I don't know what got into me. You wanted me to eat and I don't feel like it, my stomach is still upset. I don't want to fight with you anymore."

Sammie: "I don't want to fight with you either, especially not now and not like that anymore. Suzie, we have to learn a new way to have arguments besides throwing things. Sergeant Devane told me if they are called here again they will arrest me. I can't let that happen, what would happen to the boys. This could get serious because of your age."

Suzie: "I know baby, we really need to figure out some way to have our arguments without throwing things. This was my fault, I threw first. I'm so sorry."

Sammie: "I am too. Let's promise each other that we won't throw things anymore and that when we don't agree on something that we talk about it and work it out. I can't afford to go to jail."

Suzie: "We can do that. I certainly don't want you to go to jail."

Sammie: "That neighbor needs to learn to mind her own business also. I don't know why she thinks she needs to interfere when it's none of her business."

Suzie: "I agree. I figured out that it is Sergeant Devane who is telling my father that I've been here so much. I'm going to have to watch more closely to make sure I'm not being followed. He seemed to know too much for someone who has been out of town to work. We are just going to have to be more careful."

Sammie: "Yes we are and let's promise each other that we won't fight like that anymore. Besides always having to buy new dishes all the time is not good either."

Of course they made up and she actually did manage to eat a slice of pizza even though he wanted her to eat more, but he left it alone, he did not want to upset her again. For the first time ever, they sat together on the sofa and watched a movie on the television. Neither one really liked television very much but it was a good way to calm down. The movie was funny, served to lighten the mood. Sammie had slid down on the sofa and had his head resting on Suzie's lap. He put his ear to her stomach.

Sammie: "What did you say?"

Suzie: "I didn't say anything."

Sammie: "Not you, the baby just told me to stop upsetting you."

Suzie: "You are talking to the baby?"

Sammie: "No, the baby is talking to me. He doesn't like to hear you yelling."

They laughed at each other, Suzie thought that was so sweet and cute. Even though they had fought, the rest of the afternoon and evening was good. She always managed to get a very good night's sleep when she stayed with Sammie, especially with all the stuff that was going on at home.

Chapter 26

The week was going to go quickly since Suzie had a lot to do that week and they would only be able to see each other occasionally, but they could spend the weekend together. On Wednesday she went to get Sammie to go to the doctor who assured them that everything was going well and she was starting into her third month. She had lost weight which was not good and he wanted her to eat better. She told him she couldn't because she kept getting sick. She was told to drink plenty of fluids and when she wasn't nauseous to eat. She said she would and knew she would be forced to eat because Sammie was right there when he said it. The due date was still Christmas time, so much for that Vegas wedding. Suzie also knew that Sammie was upset that she couldn't be with him all the time so he could watch and take care of her. But there was nothing they could do about that at the moment.

The next couple of days, Suzie was very busy at work and had to drive to Berkeley with Kim to check things out there which should have been exciting, but wasn't. She did not like doing secretarial work but had decided that this would at least give her the opportunity to get a decent job that paid more than the drug store. Sammie did not want her to work toward the end of the pregnancy nor after the baby was born. Where they were planning on living there was no child care options and it was not going to be possible for his mother to take care of the baby.

Friday night was a late night at work and she had to work Sunday morning but was off Saturday. That was going to work well because they had to get the boys Sunday afternoon. There was still another week before her father came home and that was good.

Their weekend together was good. There were no more fights and when they did disagree they utilized the coffee table. Suzie hated that table, but it did serve a purpose. She liked spending as much time as she could with Sammie. They were good together and she liked wearing her ring. The worst part of being with Sammie was that the time always seemed to go too quickly.

Saturday night they had Kim and Gary over. With the exception of not being able to wear her ring, it was a lot of fun. Suzie was grateful that she did not get sick while they were together and it was just how it should be, friends having fun together. Kim told Suzie when she followed her into the kitchen that Sammie really loved her, it was so obvious and Gary has mentioned the same thing. It was a good evening and they each vowed to repeat these get togethers as often as they could.

After Suzie worked Sunday morning, they left for Sammie's moms. The boys were happy to see Suzie and she them. It had been two days since she had gotten sick and was hoping that part was over. His mom inquired about how things were going and they assured her that things were fine. She really hadn't noticed that Sammie had been a little quiet since the night before. They talked, laughed and ate. His mom was a fantastic cook and Suzie enjoyed eating there. She helped his mom clean up and they had to leave. Suzie would have to go to her home that night since the boys were home. They were chatterboxes all the way to their house. Sammie had grown even quieter and Suzie noticed it more now. She looked at him quizzically and he just shook his head. She guessed she would find out what was wrong sooner or later.

The following couple of weeks were very busy. Suzie was covering shifts for one of her coworkers due to vacations. They could not spend much time together so she was going to surprise him one night and stop by the house. They had talked on the phone but he was still pretty quiet and when she inquired, all he told her was that nothing was wrong.

She got off at six one evening and drove to his house. It seemed as though he wasn't there or so she thought. The boys came downstairs and told her that he was there and that she should go down the road for a few minutes and come back. She did that, let herself in and found him sitting in the living room. She asked what was wrong but he wouldn't talk to her, he just sat there watching the television. What was going on? She kept asking and he continued to not answer her so instead of fighting she left. This really upset her, what was going on? Everything had seemed fine until a week ago and not having a clue what this was all about, she went home.

She managed to eat something without getting sick and just spent some time around the house picking up and cleaning the meager furnishings, anything to keep her mind off of Sammie. She waited for him to call but he didn't which served to infuriate her. What was going on? It was getting late so she went to bed. She laid there going over all of their conversations of the past week and still could not figure it out. She then wondered if it had something to do with the other two kids. He usually talked to her about it but this time he was remaining silent. Her father was due home that weekend so they couldn't see each other and she would just have to go on. She wondered if he didn't want her around any longer. Oh, God, this was not the way to solve problems. What would she do, rather, what would they do? She was not alone any longer, she had a baby to think about.

Chapter 27

It was a couple of days before she was able to speak with him again because her father was home and would be back and forth for the next week or so. This was going to be difficult because she knew something was seriously wrong. Just before she left for work one day the phone rang. Thinking it was Sammie she answered it but it wasn't him, it was his mother. What? His mother told her that Sammie was extremely upset about everything that was going on. He didn't like that she couldn't be with him all the time because he was worried about her getting sick, losing so much weight, sleeping and if she was eating. He was also worried about how her father was going to react when they finally confronted him with their news because he knew that her father could have him arrested. He was also very depressed about not being able to see the other two kids. Suzie told her that she understood all of this, but instead of acting like a jerk, he should at least talk to her. His mother told her to just give him a little time and asked her to promise that she wouldn't leave him. She said again that he has been so much better since she came into his life and he's happier than he had been in a long time. Suzie was even more upset by what his mother had said. She couldn't figure out what his mother meant by him being better since meeting her. This was a little perplexing but she was more irritated that he talked to his mother and not to her. This just did not seem right, nothing seemed right but she had to stop thinking about it and get to work.

It would be two more days before she could talk to him. She spent those two days so sick and upset that she could not eat or drink much of anything. She knew this was not good, but she just couldn't even stomach the thought of food. Her father had not said much to her but she knew that something was on his mind also. God, she wished she was 18 and could just leave all this mess. Not knowing what to do and not having Sammie to talk to only served to make things more difficult. When she got home from work, her father was already there and he was packing a bag. Obviously he was leaving again and that was a blessing. He told her that he was going to be away for about the next two weeks and maybe longer. He then told her to go to the living room he had to talk to her.

> Jim: "I know you have been seeing Sammie this whole time. I don't like it, he is too old for you. I almost told you that if you continued to see him I would have him arrested for statutory rape and you know I can do it. But, you will be starting college soon and you have been working a lot so I'm going to leave it alone for now."

> Suzie: "Yes, I have been seeing Sammie and I really care for him. I don't want to stop seeing him."

> Jim: "I will leave it alone for now, just don't get too serious. You have your whole life ahead of you. I will be gone for about two more weeks and I know you will see him but keep in mind what I told you."

Suzie promised she would remember what he said but it was obvious that he did not know what was really going on and for now, that was a blessing. He left her more money and was gone. She did not have to work the next day and decided enough was enough. She called Sammie at work and he told her to go to the house. What was this, he didn't ask any longer, now he was telling her what to do? After she mentioned that to him she hung up the phone.

She got to his house before he did and the boys, as always, were glad to see her. They told her they were going down the street and would be home later. She asked if they were eating there and they told her yes. She told them that was good as long as their father knew where they were. They assured her he knew and left. The house was eerily quiet. Suzie went into the bedroom to get her ring, it wasn't there and that upset her.

She heard the door open and heard Sammie come up the stairs. He looked tired and quite a bit older than he had the last time she saw him. He lightly kissed her on the cheek and handed her the ring.

> Sammie: "I figured you would be looking for this. I just needed something of yours to keep with me these last few days."

Suzie: "You know, you told me in the very beginning that a relationship was built on communicating and honesty, neither of which have you been doing much of lately. I want to know what is going on."

Sammie: "I know and I'm sorry. I am so worried about you and our baby. You are not eating as you should, you are losing weight, not sleeping and you get so sick I just hate that you aren't here. I don't like it that the kids didn't get to switch this year. I haven't seen Cara and Jack in so long and it really hurts. I am also concerned about telling your father about the baby."

Suzie: "I understand all of that and I know how much you miss the kids but you have to share this with me and not keep it to yourself. I also did not appreciate your mom calling me. I really like her and under any other circumstances I would love to have talked to her but you should have been the one telling me this stuff, not her."

Sammie: "I didn't think she would call you. She asked me if you were upset and I told her that you were. When she asked if I had talked to you and I told her no, she raised hell with me."

Suzie: "Good, you deserved it. We can't make this work if we don't talk. What about our baby and what about me? She told me that you were also upset about the baby. It makes me think that you don't want us anymore."

Sammie: "Oh Suzie, that's not true. I love you so much. This was just all very overwhelming and the thought of putting you in the position we are going to be facing in a few weeks just upset me even more. I know this is going to be hard when we tell your father and I can't even begin to imagine how he is going to react. I even thought about taking you and the boys and just leaving but we can't do that. I have the house and my job. I just wish we could."

Suzie told Sammie about what her father had told her that afternoon but it didn't seem to settle him as it hadn't settled her either. Her heart went out to him because of the kids, and she wondered how a mother could keep kids away from their father. She just didn't understand that but then she thought about the last time her father had seen her brother. She vowed to herself that no matter what the situation was when she got married, she would do whatever she had to do to make it work for the kids. If things were that bad after they grew up, then she would make changes because she just hated seeing him hurt so much.

She ran to the bathroom and he was right there with her as she was violently ill. He sat on the tub rubbing her back hating that she was going through this. They thought it would be over soon but it seemed to be getting worse. When she finished, he carried her to the living room and gently placed her on the sofa. It was apparent that she was extremely weak. He sat next to her.

Sammie: "When was the last time you ate something?"

Suzie: "Honestly? About two days ago. I was so worried about us and what you were doing that I just couldn't face food. I've been so sick also that just the thought of food made me nauseous."

Sammie: "Damn it, you know you are supposed to eat. Neither you nor the baby are going to do well if you don't eat. I'm going to fix something for dinner, I know the boys aren't home and after they go to bed we are going to talk. We are fine, I promise and I don't want you to worry about it anymore. Now you stay here and rest while I go fix us something to eat. Suzie, I love you."

Suzie: "I love you too but I'm still a bit angry with you."

He figured out that she was feeling weak, but she was sure he didn't know just how weak she felt. She heard him rummaging through the kitchen trying to come up with something that she could eat. He didn't have much as he had not been shopping so he decided to make her pancakes and sausage. That would be fairly easy to eat and she should keep that down. Suzie fell asleep. He checked on her and saw that she was sleeping and smiled, he loved her so much and he promised himself that he would not make her feel insecure again. God, how he wished that she was older, everything would be so much easier.

Suzie woke to the smell of sausage cooking but she did not feel like moving, besides she was actually feeling much weaker and was a little concerned. She hated feeling like this and thought that it was going to be about six more months before this would be over, but then she would have someone else to worry about. At 17, was she really capable of handling all this? She turned her head and closed her eyes again.

Sammie brought her food to her, insisting she sit up and eat something. He knew this was not the best dinner but she had to eat. She picked at her food until he

152

decided to feed her and it actually felt good to get food in her stomach. Maybe she should try to start eating better since it seemed to make her feel a bit better.

The boys were not due home for another hour so they started talking.

Sammie: "Suzie, I am so sorry about the way I've been acting. I know I scared you and I had promised to never do that again. I just got overwhelmed."

Suzie: "Sammie, I understand, but when you don't talk to me it makes me feel like you don't want me and the baby, I was really worried. What would I do without you?"

Sammie: "I know baby and I can't tell you how sorry I am. I do love you and I do love this little one, I have no excuse except that sometimes I can be a jerk. I'm also sorry that I called my mother but I needed to talk to someone and at that moment it was more about the other kids than you and the baby. Plus, I didn't want to upset you any more than you already have been lately. She gave me hell for not talking to you also."

Suzie: "Yeah, I was a little shook up when she called me. I like her and I know you need someone to talk to, I get it. I have Jean and she has been a godsend but these past few days she wasn't sure what to say to me. It's been hard. I know we are going to have ups and downs, everyone does but if we can't turn to each other to solve issues then what are we doing together?"

Sammie: "God, sometimes you are so much wiser than your years. Suzie, I do love you and I promise I will not do this again. If anything is bothering me I will talk to you. I know you will do the same, you always have. Are you feeling any better? I can always tell when you aren't feeling well."

Suzie: "Yes, I am feeling better now. I do not like feeling like this at all."

Sammie took her in his arms and asked if she forgave him. She said yes and then told him she was off the next day but knew she couldn't stay that night. Sammie told her she could and she looked at him quite surprised. Ok, how do we explain this to the boys? Sammie told her not to worry about it, he would take care of them. She then said that the next day she would go and get some things to cook all of them something special for dinner since she was off. He smiled and they just sat there holding each other.

Chapter 28

The next morning Suzie heard the kids getting up and Sammie getting ready for work. She stayed in the bedroom, not exactly sure how the boys were going to react to her being there since this was the first time she had stayed there with the boys home. She couldn't wait any longer and tried to quietly get to the bathroom. Sam spotted her and just gave her that glaring stare he had, shit, she didn't want to have to explain anything. She heard Sammie call him and she just went into the bathroom. When she came out they were nowhere in sight and Sammie was waiting for her in the bedroom. After telling her to have a fun day, he handed her $50 to get groceries for the dinner she had promised to cook that night. He kissed her goodbye and he was off.

She got dressed quickly, did a quick make up job, made the bed and went out to the kitchen to find some coffee. The boys came out from their rooms and just looked at her which made her feel a little funny. She told them they were going to cook dinner tonight but had to go to the store and asked if they wanted to go. They said no, so she thought it just best to leave.

After shopping, the boys heard the car and opened the garage door so she could pull in. After closing the door, they carried the groceries upstairs. Smiling she thought this was going to be great if things stayed this way forever. They set about preparing dinner. It seemed they used every pot in the kitchen but they sure had a lot of fun. Suzie had also bought things to make a strawberry shortcake for dessert and they made an even bigger mess preparing the cake. She called them both over to her, told them to close their eyes and open their mouths. They did so through fits of giggling and she filled both of their mouths with whipped cream. Their eyes shot open and they couldn't swallow fast enough so they could laugh. It was a great day and she really felt that they were going to get along just fine. Of course, being boys they did not want to help clean up so Suzie told them to set the table and she would take care of the mess.

Since they didn't have to put the dinner in the oven yet, they spent time talking together and they showed her things they had in their rooms. Sam had not come back and when she went to use the rest room, she heard him singing along with the music he had playing. She stopped to listen for a minute and thought he had a really good voice. She was impressed.

When it was time to get dinner in the oven, she did so and filled the pot with water for the spaghetti. At least the kitchen had gotten cleaned up. Boy, they could sure make a mess. She heard the front door open and Sammie come up the stairs. He had a smile that could kill on his face. He came to her and kissed her sweetly, hollered down the hall to the boys. This was surely domestic bliss. He went to take a shower as she finished up the dinner. She called the boys to help put the food on the table and pour their drinks. They seemed to like to help and she enjoyed the time they had spent together. She did not see Sammie leaning against the wall watching what was happening but his smile told her that he approved. Everyone seemed really happy and content.

They ate the luscious dinner and everyone enjoyed it. Veal cutlet parmigiana, spaghetti and a fresh garden salad. Part way through the dinner, Suzie ran to the restroom again. She heard the boys asking each other if they were going to get sick too. Sammie went out and assured them they wouldn't. They asked why Suzie was getting sick all the time and he just told them that she had been through a lot lately and would be feeling better soon.

While eating desert, the boys giggled remembering the whipped cream that got shot in their mouths. Sammie looked at them all inquisitively but no one offered an explanation. He was just going to have to get used to the secrets these three and soon to be four were going to have. They all enjoyed the dinner and Sammie told the boys to clean up the kitchen. Suzie could stay one more day but then would have to leave. She asked Sammie if she could take the boys for lunch before she left and Sammie told her that was fine.

Everything seemed to settle into a good place. Sammie was more like he had been previously and that pleased Suzie. She told him there was enough sauce left over if he wanted to use it for their dinner the following night. He did not want her to go but it was getting closer to when they were going to talk to her father so he didn't want to push her or cause any trouble.

They spent the evening talking about where they were headed.

Suzie: "Sammie I am really starting to worry about talking to my father. He could cause a great deal of trouble for us."

Sammie: "I've been thinking about it also and I think I have an idea. We want to tell him over Labor Day weekend. So, I thought we could have a cookout, invite him, my mother, the boys, Kim and Gary. I think it would be better to have a lot of people around and he may not react too horribly."

Suzie: "You know, that sounds good. It just may work."

Sammie: "You know I honestly thought of just taking off with all of you but we can't do that, like I said before. It just wouldn't be right."

Suzie: "No, that wouldn't be a good thing. But, your idea just may work."

Sammie: "Hey, have you given any thought to what you want to name the baby?"

Suzie: "I have. When I was growing up in Petersville there was a guy who lived next door to me who was more like a big brother than a friend. His name was Jonathan and about a year ago he was killed in a car accident. Since there is already a Sam, I thought that Jonathan would be a nice name if it's a boy."

Sammie: "That sounds good and I do like that. So if it's a boy, then Jonathan it will be."

Suzie: "If it's a girl, I have always loved the name Patricia. I have a cousin with that name and I just always loved it."

Sammie: "I like that also, so Patricia or Jonathan it is."

Suzie: "Don't you have any ideas?"

Sammie: "Since you already have their first names picked out and I really like them both maybe I'll come up with a middle name that we both like."

The boys came from their rooms to tell them goodnight. This whole entire couple of days seemed so amazingly easy, everything was going to work for them. The biggest hurdle would be telling her father, but since she was already pregnant and would be almost five months when they told him, what could he say. They were going to have a baby and surely he wouldn't have him put in jail. This was going to work.

The following morning Suzie woke up before Sammie and ran to the bathroom. She did not think she woke him but she had and he was right there with her. She was seriously getting tired of getting sick. She told Sammie that the following week they had a doctor appointment. She knew she had lost more weight and he was not going to be happy about that. What could she do, she just couldn't eat. While Sammie got ready for work, Suzie made his breakfast and some coffee. She knew he would have a fit if he caught her drinking coffee so she took small sips from his cup and refilled it thinking he wouldn't know, but he was standing there watching her. Oh shit. He just smiled and shook his head. They ate breakfast and the boys came out to join them. They ate also and without even being asked, cleaned up the kitchen.

Suzie told them that after she took a shower and cleaned up around the house a bit, they were going to go for lunch before she had to leave. They did not like the idea that she was going to leave because they both made faces. She told them she had to go to work, which she did.

She took them to A&W for lunch. She loved watching them watch the girls on their roller skates. Boys, do they ever stop looking, she laughed to herself. They had a good time and then they had to go home. Suzie told them that in a couple of weeks when she had some extra time off work, she was going to treat them to something special. She made them promise her that they would be really good and help their dad with dinner and cleaning up between now and then. They promised they would. She took them home and was very surprised when Teddy leaned over and kissed her on the cheek. "I really like you" he told her. She smiled and assured him she felt the same way about them. She wouldn't be able to see them for a few days and she would miss them.

Chapter 29

The next week went quickly, work was busy and her father was appearing more often. One night after she had just gotten home and had gone to bed, he woke her up telling her he had someone he wanted her to meet. She got up, went to the kitchen and saw Betty. She knew Betty from years before when she was little and wasn't surprised in the least to see her. While growing up in Petersville, her parents owned a three-family house. They lived in the bottom apartment, Betty and her family lived on the third floor. They had known each other since Suzie was about five. She knew they had been seeing each other through the years and now that her mother was gone she knew Betty was going to be around. That was fine, she liked Betty. After talking for a while, she went back to bed.

When she went back to bed she could not help thinking that very soon she was going to be starting her fifth month and was really wondering what her father was going to say. While lying there with her hand on her stomach, she felt a slight flutter. She jumped up wondering what had happened when she realized that it was the baby. Oh my God, she so wanted to be with Sammie when that happened the first time. Suddenly it was all real. She had felt their child moving around inside of her and she couldn't help but cry happy tears. She couldn't wait to tell Sammie. She would be up early enough to call him before he went to work.

When she called Sammie and told him, she could hear him choke up a little. He was really excited and it was only a few more days before they saw the doctor. Suzie was starting to feel a bit excited about this and she really wanted to tell Kim but they had promised each other they would not tell anyone else until Labor Day when everyone would find out. The weekend was coming and she wanted to spend it with Sammie and knew that she could because her father was working that big job again and would not be home. Besides, this made her feel even closer to Sammie, their child was real, it was moving.

This was all working out better than they had thought. The weekend together was wonderful. Saturday night the boys were staying at their friend's down the street and that was going to work because she wanted to be alone with Sammie. During the afternoon his mom had called to see how she was doing. His mom told her again how happy she was that she was in her son's life and that she had been shopping for the baby. She seemed genuinely happy about them, his father was a different story. For the most part when Suzie was at their house, he just sat and stared at her. Sammie told her that he was just like that and don't let it bother her so she didn't think much about it.

Saturday night was magical. Sammie was definitely back to his romantic self which she was more than getting used to. They had a lazy Sunday morning. Neither of them wanted to get up so they didn't, they stayed in bed and talked about where they were going to put the baby, the things they were going to need, and giggled over who was going to get up in the middle of the night when the baby cried. For one fleeting second, she thought, God I'm only 17 years old and dealing with all of this, but then she looked up at Sammie and all her doubts and fears fell away.

They heard the front door open, the boys bounding up the stairs as Sammie jumped out of bed and ran to shut the door just in time. She also realized that she had not been sick at all that weekend. Finally, maybe this stuff was over. If this happened to everyone why do women keep having babies?

They lazily got dressed and went out to the living room and just wanted to hang around the house that day. She told the boys that one day during the week she would pick them up and go to lunch again, that excited them. She also told them that the following week she had a huge surprise for them because there was not much time left of summer and she thought they deserved to do something special.

On that Tuesday, they went to the doctor. He was not pleased that Suzie had lost more weight. She told him and so did Sammie that she had not been able to eat because she kept getting sick. She also told him that for the last four days, she had not been sick and had been able to eat. He then told her that if that had not happened, he would have put her on bed rest. Oh shit, she couldn't do that. She was well into the fourth month and the baby was growing fine, but she would definitely have to eat regularly from now on. She was also going to start showing with the next month. With all well, she took Sammie back to work. He had been so good about everything, paying all the bills and buying anything she needed. How did she get so lucky?

It was going to start getting busy at work as they stocked a lot of back to school supplies and there were not many stores in the town so most went to the drug store to get the things they needed. Suzie had been given some extra hours which was fine since she was going to need some extra money. Jean had been watching her closely and she knew that. The days at work flew by but she had managed to take the boys for their lunch at A&W one day and next week she had her special treat for them. They were such good kids and had suddenly stopped asking so many questions. She really felt like they knew more than they were letting on but decided she was not going to worry about it.

She could not go to Sammie's that weekend. Her father had called her and told her they were going to be at Columns for dinner and for her to meet them there when she got off of work. She said fine and went back to work, but wondered throughout the day why her father wanted her to meet them at the restaurant. Maybe it was nothing and they just wanted to have dinner with her. She hated the weekends she couldn't spend with Sammie.

After work she went to Columns, a nice restaurant with good food. They had dinner and it was nice. She went to play the jukebox and saw this guy she had met once before, his name was Stan and she really did not think much about him and could have cared less at that point. He spoke to her and she did stop to talk for a moment. She noticed her father watching her and smiling, she should have known what he was up to. Stan was friendly but quiet. She just talked to him for a little while and that was it. She was not interested.

Her father asked her about him when she got back to the table, she told him she had met him in there one other time previously. Her father then told her that he had talked to him a few times when he had been in there and he seemed nice. She didn't think anything else about it. Betty stayed at the house that weekend and Suzie was grateful for the heavy work schedule. They told her that they were going to steam clams Saturday night and have some other special foods. Suzie said alright but she did not like clams or seafood for that matter. She supposed it would be fun so she just went about her business. Sammie stopped in the store on Saturday. He was dressed for work and told her he had worked that day because someone had called in sick. She told him she would have to wait until Sunday night when her father left to take Betty home to get over to the house. He was okay with that, he said he had some things to take care of at the house that he had been letting go.

Time seemed to go quickly the rest of the night and when she got home it was evident that they had been drinking. Suzie just made a soda. They tried to get her to eat a clam and she refused but she did eat some of the shrimp which was good. Her father was a good cook. They laughed and had a good time. Neither one noticed that she had put on some weight. If she laid on her back you could just begin to feel a little baby bump, but that little bump wasn't going to be little much longer. They did have a good time and then Suzie went to bed.

She had to work early the next day until one in the afternoon. She went to Sammie's after work knowing her father had taken Betty home. She was just glad to see him but he seemed a little quiet. She asked what was wrong and he led her to the sofa while he sat on the coffee table.

Sammie: "I just hate it that we can't be together like we should be. This is getting harder and harder. The kids are asking why you can't stay all the time."

Suzie: "I know, it is difficult but we are going to tell my father in a couple of weeks. I really believe with everyone around he's going to be okay with everything. It's going to be rough but we will get through it. He knows I've been seeing you, just not quite how much."

Sammie: "I agree, but I am getting nervous. I want you here with me and the boys. We are a family. Well we are going to be a family and we should be together. I worry when you aren't here if you are eating, sleeping and are you still getting sick?"

Suzie: "Yes, I am eating, maybe not as much as I should but I am. Sleeping is difficult because I have gotten used to falling asleep in your arms and no, I haven't been sick in about two weeks."

Sammie: "Good, can you still feel the baby moving?"

Suzie: "Yes, especially at night when I am laying still. It moves a lot now and I have a feeling that this baby is going to keep us awake a lot."

Sammie: "I can't wait until I can feel it move."

Sammie laid his hand on her stomach, kissed her gently, and told her how much he loved her. If only things had continued that way.

Suzie: "Can I take the boys somewhere special during the week? I have a day off and would love to take them to the zoo across the river. They have been so good and deserve a special treat."

Sammie: "I suppose you can but don't spoil them. Are you going to need some money?"

Suzie: "No, I'm good, this is my treat. Sammie, are things going to be this good forever?"

Sammie: "No, they are going to be better because you won't have to leave."

Suzie: "It will be really nice but I'm still nervous about the baby. I have babysat, but I don't really know what we will do with a baby all the time."

Sammie: "We will figure it all out and you know I will help you when I'm home. Everything is going to be perfect."

She knew that his birthday was coming and she wanted to take the boys shopping for presents for him. She would have to sneak them off one afternoon. That would be fun, they could make a cake and have a little party. She smiled and even smiled more when he put his hand on her stomach. With that, the baby moved and she giggled.

The next day went quickly at work and she was glad. Jean had scheduled several make overs so they were busy. It was fun doing the make overs and for a fleeting moment Suzie thought it was sad that she wouldn't be able to take advantage of Estee's generous offer. She thought she would rather do make overs and stage make up than take shorthand.

She met her father at Columns again for dinner that night and again Stan was there. She still was not the least bit interested and tried to act that way, but he kept looking at her which bothered her. She just ignored him and enjoyed her dinner. Her father seemed fine and he also seemed happy. He told her that he would be gone for about another week and she said that was fine. He also told her that night that he was going to put the house up for sale and find something in town to rent. She understood that it was probably better that way. It was still hard to go to the house.

Chapter 30

The next morning Suzie picked up the boys early and they were off. Of course, they argued about who was sitting in the front so Suzie flipped a coin. Sam won for the trip to the zoo. They had no idea where they were going and of course asked constantly if they were there yet. Silly kids, but she could remember doing the same thing not too long ago. When they got to the zoo, they were beyond excited. Suzie told them the rules for outings with her again and they agreed. The day went very quickly and they had a fabulous time. Sam made a face when he had to get in the back seat for the ride home, but that was the deal. Suzie told them on the way home that their father's birthday was coming soon and she was going to get them Friday morning so they could go shopping for presents. That excited them.

When they got to the house, Sammie was already home and cooking hot dogs with a salad. Suzie did not have the heart to tell him that she hated hot dogs, she would eat them, besides he couldn't screw that up too much. The boys were so excited they were both talking at once and Sammie was laughing. Then they ran off making the sounds of some of the animals they had seen. She was going to have to find out when their birthdays were so she could plan something special for them. Because of the situation this past year she was not able to celebrate anything with them, but it would be different this year. If only Suzie knew how true that was.

Sammie was pleased that they were getting along so well, he just missed the other two kids and wished they could all be together. Maybe someday they would be. Suzie stayed that night and the kids were getting used to her being around more because she noticed that Sam did not give her that glaring 'mad' look anymore. She thought it was kind of cute but was glad that he seemed to be warming up to her. Teddy on the other hand was around her as much as possible.

Suzie worked the next day and only saw them for a little while. She had to go home and do some things her father had asked her to do. That was fine because the next morning she was taking the boys shopping, this would be an adventure. She knew the kind of clothes that Sammie liked already deciding that she would let the boys pick out what they wanted for him and she would add something to it from her. His birthday was the following week and they promised to keep the presents hidden at the house. They would spend the day cooking another meal and making him a cake. This was going to be fun.

She took them to a men's store she knew of in the neighboring town. The boys picked out purple, yes purple jeans, a black and purple belt and Suzie picked a white shirt with a purple print on it. It actually looked good together, but purple? The weekend after his birthday they were having a cook out at Kim's and she figured he would wear that outfit. He was going to take the kids to his Mom's for that weekend so they could have a weekend before they planned on sharing their news.

Suzie made sure she was off the day of his birthday and spent the day at the house with the boys fixing the dinner and baking him a cake. They had such fun making the cake and the laughter was contagious. Suzie had the stereo up pretty loud and they were singing along with the music. She liked Elvis and had some of her records playing when she stopped a minute to listen to Sam. He really did have an amazing voice even at his age. They made a holy mess in the kitchen and they did not hear Sammie come up the stairs. He was standing in the doorway smiling as he watched Suzie and his boys dancing around the kitchen. The boys turned around to see him standing there and he put his finger to his lips to keep them quiet, but Suzie noticed the difference in the mood and turned around. They were laughing and Sammie asked what was going on.

They had a great dinner, he was very surprised when they brought out his cake and sang Happy Birthday to him. She could just see the love in his eyes and, oh, how she loved him. This was such fun and the boys had a great time. They brought out his presents and he opened them very slowly. It was driving the boys crazy but he drew it out just to tease them a bit. He liked the gifts. It was a great day and Suzie just imagined how it would be the following year with a little baby around. She was getting more excited about the baby and really wanted to share this with the boys but it wasn't time yet. After cleaning up the holy mess, the boys went off to their rooms.

It was one of the very few times that Suzie could remember them laughing and really being happy. She wondered why that was and just figured it was because of their mom leaving with the other two kids. Her heart sank, thinking about Sammie missing them so much.

She had to work the following day but was staying with him that night. She would be able to go back for the weekend. Sammie was taking the boys to his mom's after work on Friday and she would be there after the store closed that night. His birthday night was wonderful and he kept telling her over and over again how much he loved her. She told him the same thing because in her heart and soul, she did love him more than anything else in the world.

Chapter 31

Suzie arrived at the house after work and he was standing in the driveway with the garage door open. She pulled in and he went right to her after closing the door, picking her up gently to carry her up the stairs. The music was already playing, the house was clean, and he had candles lit in every room. She loved this romantic side of him. They sat on the sofa and talked for quite a while. There was another doctor appointment coming up this week and she would be in her fifth month. She was going to start to really show soon and Labor Day weekend was fast approaching. This would all be over then and she could be where she really wanted to be. Everything was going to be perfect, or so she thought. He laid his hand on her stomach and started talking to the baby which he did frequently. He also sang to the baby which she really liked. He would soon be able to feel the baby kicking and moving, the flutters she had been feeling were getting stronger. They also had noticed that her waist had thickened a bit and if she laid on her back, they could feel the baby bump.

Suzie: "Whatever this baby is, a boy or a girl, I hope it has your hair and your eyes. I love your eyes and I love the color of your hair."

Sammie: "No, I want it to have your eyes, you have stunning eyes and if it has dark hair which it should since we both have dark hair it will either be extremely handsome or exceptionally beautiful as its mother is."

Suzie: "I just don't want to get fat. I see some women come in the store after they have their babies and they are huge. Jean said she had some exercises I can do after that will help get rid of the tummy. I want you with me when it's born. I'm going to be scared to death."

Sammie: "I know baby, I will be right by your side. Haven't I been all along?"

Suzie: "Yes, you have been amazing. I can't wait until Kim knows. I really hate keeping things from her."

Sammie: "I know, but it was better this way so there was no chance of your father finding out. Do you still like the names you picked out?"

Suzie: "Yes, have you thought about middle names yet?

Sammie: "Yes I have. How about Jonathan Arthur for our son or Patricia Lynn for our daughter?"

Suzie: "I love both names. Amazingly, my cousin's middle name is Lynn, that's pretty cool that you thought of that name."

Sammie: "Well, right now I have something else on my mind."

He smiled at her and she knew that the rest of the night was theirs and theirs alone. That weekend it seemed like all the problems that had gone on with her parents, the rape and all the other bad stuff was in a different life time. She was on the cusp of entering a new adventure with this man who loved her and who she loved. She glanced down at her ring, she knew he wanted to get her something special when they got married but with having to do it sooner she wasn't sure what was going to happen and she really didn't care about asking him at that moment either.

They were lying in bed talking.

Suzie: "I know we have talked about this before but can we wait until after I turn 18 and still go to Vegas?"

Sammie: "No, I told you why before. I don't want any issues with this baby. I have been thinking more about it. If your father gives us permission to get married, we can just slip away somewhere for the ceremony. Then, I thought you might like to have a party or reception after that. We can then invite everyone to celebrate with us."

Suzie: "That sounds like a great idea. I'm sure we could get Betty and your mom to help plan that."

Sammie: "I'm sure they would love it, I know my mother will."

Suzie: "I wish Cara and Jack could be here with us. I really wish I could have met them before now."

Sammie: "I know, I do too. Maybe we can get them here next summer."

Suzie wanted to ask more questions about him and his ex-wife but it always put him in a bad mood so she refrained, maybe someday she would find out more. She still had the definite thought that there was the story he told her, the ex wife's story, and the truth. It was the same with her parents so she decided to leave it alone.

They dressed for Kim's. Sammie wore the outfit they had purchased for his birthday and he looked great. They got to Kim's and it was a very enjoyable afternoon. Sammie and Suzie had some pictures taken and were told over and over that they made a stunning couple. The rest of the afternoon was spent talking about Kim and Gary's wedding. Oh how she wished she could share all her news with Kim. They had to leave a little early because they had to get the boys. Suzie had found out that her father was going to be in town the next day and would have to go home. She wouldn't have to do that much longer.

Suzie met her father for dinner at Columns that Monday. That guy Stan was there again and this was getting annoying. She still was not interested and her father came close to asking him to join them for dinner when Suzie kicked her father under the table so he knew not to ask. He did tell her that the house had sold and he had found another house across town that was furnished. They could move two weeks after Labor Day. There was an extra room there so they could store Suzie's furniture and extra things in that room. That sounded fine but now she was going to have to spend more time at home getting the house ready to go. She did not like that but it was necessary. Betty would be around to help her and it was going to be a busy few weeks. She really wished her father knew what was going on because he wouldn't have had to rent that house, if she was moving into Sammie's then he could just go to Betty's. Well, that would all be figured out after Labor Day.

On Tuesday, Suzie picked Sammie up and they went to the doctor. As always, Sammie was right on her heels in the office. He had to step out during the exam and he was not happy but he complied. The doctor called him back in and told them that he was happy that she was gaining weight. She had lost almost ten pounds when she had been so sick but had gained five of those back since last month. He told them the baby was on the small side but if she ate better and watched herself everything should be good. That was it and they left the office. Sammie told her when she moved in with him he would make sure she ate better than he knew she did now. She took him back to work and went home to start packing.

Chapter 32

Everything seemed to be going well. The house was almost done, Betty had been there to help quite a bit. Suzie sensed that she knew something was going on by some of the things Betty had said and Suzie just told her it was because of everything that was going on with the move and college starting soon. That seemed to appease Betty, at least for the moment. Betty also mentioned to Suzie that she had gained some weight. Suzie told her that she had been eating too much take-out food and had to stop. Once they moved it would settle down. The move would take place two weeks after Labor Day so there was still some time. Betty told her that her father would be gone for about another week or so but then would be back home. He was still working on that big IBM job. That was fine with Suzie and Betty handed her some money before she left.

Suzie spent most of her time with Sammie and everything seemed to be going really well. He was or at least he said he was getting really excited about the baby and their future. Suzie was also, although she was getting nervous about the Labor Day weekend, the big revelation. They were planning on making the invitations that week. She was worried about what her father would say, she was concerned about what the boys would think. They had been good kids that whole summer, always listening to what she told them to do and doing it without any argument. She already loved them and loved being around them. Most importantly she loved Sammie and loved every minute she spent with him.

They had planned on spending this weekend, the weekend prior to Labor Day, with the boys just hanging around and maybe going on a picnic. She was supposed to go to Sammie's after work that Saturday. She left work and was very excited even though her father had called and wanted her to meet him for dinner that night. He told her that he had to come up to the house for something but was going right back, she could go back to Sammie's after dinner. She got to the house but he was not outside which was unusual as he had always met her in the driveway. The garage was closed and she was worried that something had happened. The door was locked when she tried to open it so she used her key. It was eerily quiet in the house and pretty dark which was strange since it was only 3 o'clock in the afternoon.

She made her way up the stairs slowly. When she reached the top step, she could smell alcohol. What? Sammie didn't drink and she wondered what was going on. She did not hear the boys at all either. Before she could think another thought, Sammie came around the corner from the bedroom and punched her in the face. She tried to catch herself but couldn't and she fell down the stairs. What the hell is going on? What is he doing? She tried to ask him but he had followed her down the stairs and started to hit her repeatedly, yelling at her about how she had cheated on him. What? She had never cheated on him. She tried to say something but couldn't, all she could do was curl up in a ball until he stopped. He didn't stop though, he started kicking her. He kicked her in the stomach, in the side and as he did so, she rolled down the second stairs. She was in such shock she couldn't get any sound out of her mouth and the blows kept coming and coming. She tried to get away from him but he kept coming after her. He had kicked her again and again in the side and the stomach. She was crying and so upset she just stayed there curled in a ball. Finally, she was able to get away from him and crawl across the floor to the door to the garage. She looked up at him and the look he had on his face seared through to her soul. She was able to get up and get to her car. What had just happened? What was going on? God she hurt. She got in her car and left.

She drove up the road to the school parking lot, sat there for a bit crying so hard she couldn't see anything. That's when the cramps started. Oh my God, the baby. He had kicked her so hard in the stomach she knew he hurt the baby. What was she going to do? She knew that Jean was home so she decided to go there, she didn't have any other place to go. When she pulled in the driveway, Jean was outside and knew that something was wrong. The cramps were getting worse. What had he done?

Jean called for her husband to help her get Suzie inside. Suzie was crying and covered in blood. She told her husband to go next door and get their neighbor who was a nurse. Jean tried to clean up some of the blood where Suzie's mouth and nose were bleeding, her face was swollen and Jean could already see the bruises. She kept asking what had happened and finally Suzie was able to tell her that Sammie had hit her. 'Hit her' wasn't the word for it, he had literally beat the living hell out of her. Through her sobs and tears Suzie managed to tell her that the cramps were getting really bad. Jean looked at her with such a pitiful look, she knew what was going on.

Jean managed to get Suzie to settle down a little. The nurse came in and asked what the heck had happened to her. Jean told her and also told her that she was pregnant. The nurse told Jean to get some towels and water. She looked at Suzie and told her she was probably going to lose the baby. Oh my God, no was all Suzie could say, she put her hands on her stomach and just cried uncontrollably. The nurse tended to Suzie and it wasn't too long before she told her that the baby had been born. He was not breathing and was too small to try to save. She was holding him in her hand and Suzie mumbled that she wanted to see him.

He was so tiny. She took him in her hand and just stared at him. All she said was, 'Jonathan'. His little fingers were curled into fists, almost as if he was going to hit back to help her, his eyes were not open yet but his face was perfect. She could almost see through his skin, he was so tiny and she was supposed to have protected him. It was then that she said, "Oh my God, he killed our son." She didn't understand any of this but the nurse went to take Jonathan from her and she gently kissed her son on his forehead. She just closed her eyes and cried and cried.

She had no idea what the nurse had done with the baby and did not want to know. Jean and the nurse were trying to clean her up when they noticed the bruises. There were two foot prints on her stomach and several on her side. They asked what really hurt and Suzie said her side and lower abdomen. The nurse examined her further and found Suzie had two, maybe three cracked ribs, her pelvis was probably cracked also and there were bruises all over her face, arms and legs. Jean's husband wanted to call the police which caused Suzie to become hysterical. "No, you can't. He has two boys, the state will take them if he is arrested. You can't please, promise me." They did not call the police. They gave her a little time to calm down but she was numb. She did not know what she was supposed to do, what she was going to do, or anything, she was in shock. She had just lost her son and was supposed to meet her father for dinner, she couldn't possibly show up looking like this.

They had about an hour to try to make her presentable. Jean knew the whole situation and knew her father well enough to know that if he saw her like this, he would go after Sammie and possibly kill him. She knew her husband would react that way so she decided to help Suzie look as best as she could to get through dinner. The nurse and Jean made Suzie up with the stage make up that they used for make overs and it was working, the bruises on her face were not visible. They would be more pronounced the next day. After she was all cleaned up, Jean gave her some of her clothes to change into. She was extremely upset but if she didn't show up at Columns, her father would come looking for her. She did not want him to go to Sammie's. In a fog, she managed to drive to Column's, her father was there so she had to put on her game face. She could not even think about what had happened because she did not want to start crying again. She walked gingerly into the restaurant, her ribs hurt and it hurt to walk. How the hell was she ever going to explain this the next day? She just could not understand why the man she loved with all of her heart and soul could do something like this to her.

Her father was genuinely happy to see her but, he could see that something was wrong by the look on his face. He knew she had been seeing Sammie and he asked if she was okay. She just said that they had a fight, he was happy to hear that, if only he knew the truth. They ate dinner which was the last thing in the world Suzie wanted to do, but she had to eat enough to make him think that she was okay. He bought her a drink and she drank it. God, it was getting harder and harder for her to move, the pain was getting worse. She went to the restroom and saw that she looked pretty good but while in the stall, she looked at some of the bruises. My God, there were two footprints on her stomach, she couldn't reach up to look at her side because her side hurt too much and taking deep breaths was just not possible. How was she ever going to cover this up so her father wouldn't know what had happened? If anything happened to Sammie then the boys would have to go to the state, she couldn't be responsible if that happened. God, what was she going to do?

After they finished eating and had another drink, they decided to go home. Her father had asked about Stan, she wasn't even sure who Stan was but she told him she had talked to him a couple of times and that was it. As she followed her father home, she remembered that just before you turned slightly left to go to the house, there was an embankment straight ahead. She thought if she drove off the embankment she would surely get bruised, at least enough to cover up what Sammie had done to her. She crested the hill, saw her father veer to the left and she pushed the gas pedal and held her beloved Mustang straight. She felt herself go over the edge and the car rolled twice. It landed on its roof, thankfully she did not have her seat belt on or she would have died when the roof came crashing down, although at the moment, that seemed like a pretty good idea. She put the car in park, turned it off and cried herself to sleep from the shock of what had happened. This must be a nightmare was her last thought.

Sometime later, she would find out that it had been over an hour, she felt herself being tugged from the car. She woke up to her father pulling her from the car and crying, as he asked what had happened and if she was alright. She said she didn't know, she pressed the brakes but it was like they let loose and yes she was alright but hurt a lot. He got her from the car and held her for dear life which was excruciating. He told her he did not know where she had gone, she was right behind him and then she was gone. He thought she went to Sammie's and he went there looking for her. Oh shit, so now he knew something was wrong. Good, after what he had done to her he deserved to worry.

Her father told her that he was coming back home when he saw something shine in the woods and got out of his truck to see what it was, and that's when he found her. Of course, the police came and it was her favorite cop, Sgt. Devane asking if she was okay and what had happened. She said she was fine, just sore and that

179

when she tried to use the brakes they just didn't work. Thankfully it was dark so no one could see the bruises that had already started to make an appearance. The tow truck came to pull her car from the embankment. They asked if she wanted to go to the hospital, she said no, she just wanted to go home.

Finally after what seemed like an eternity, they went home. She wanted to go to bed. She wanted to be alone but her father insisted that they had to call her mother, now that attention she didn't need. He did and she talked to her mother and told her she was okay, but of course the first thing her mother asked was if she was drunk. She told her no that the brakes seemed to let go, she told her she just wanted to go to bed, she would talk to her later. She could hear her father yelling at her mother on the phone as Suzie made her way to her room stopping in the restroom to remove all the makeup.

She took one look in the mirror and went limp, her lower lip was swollen, there was evidence of blood on her mouth and her nose, both of her eyes were swollen and since she had removed the makeup she could see they were already blackening. Very slowly and gingerly she removed her clothes. On her right side, there were numerous bruises and that's what really hurt. The nurse must be right, she must have some cracked ribs. There were more bruises on her side by her hip, on her leg but the ones that were the worse were the two footprints on her stomach, the stomach that hours ago had held their child. He killed their son. How would she ever get over this?

She heard a light knock, shut the light off and opened the door. She still did not want her father to see her. He asked if she was okay and did she want to go to the hospital. She said no, she just wanted to sleep. She asked if her car was ruined and he told her he would go and check it out the next day. She shook her head and slowly closed her door, just wanting to be alone. As she was trying to find a comfortable position to lay down in she heard her father talking to Betty on the phone from his room. She didn't care anymore, she didn't care about anything, she cried and cried until she shook, how could he do this to her. He had never, ever raised a hand to her previously, what the hell had happened? Then she thought of Jonathan. My poor baby was all she thought. With her body shaking from crying so hard, she dozed off from sheer exhaustion.

Chapter 33

She did not wake up until late the next morning, the ringing phone roused her. She knew it was Sammie but he was the last person she wanted to talk to. She heard her father tell him that she was still sleeping and asked him what he had done to her. She slowly tried to move in the bed and with every move, the pain was searing. She looked at her arms, legs and stomach and saw all the bruises. When she finally was able to stand she looked in her mirror. Oh my God, she looked like she had been a punching bag, her face was bruised and swollen, and her side was killing her as was her pelvis. She looked down and saw the footprints. All she could think of was that he killed their son and the images of their son that were now burned in her memory seemed crystal clear. What had happened? She could not understand what had caused him to do this to her. How could he do this? He was always so sweet and good with her, what the hell had happened. She started crying again.

She heard her father going down the stairs and went to the bathroom very slowly. She wanted to take a shower, she felt like she was covered in grime and of course, from the miscarriage, she was bleeding. She heard the phone ring as she stepped into the tub and let it ring. Her father did not answer it either, she did not know where he was and she didn't care. She tried so hard to wash the memories away as she showered. She couldn't, she leaned against the wall and cried. She thought back to every move she had made when she first got to Sammie's and remembered the smell of alcohol. Had he been drinking? She never saw him drink except a glass of wine with dinner one night. She also had never smelled alcohol on him. Then her thoughts turned to the boys, oh my God, were they alright? If he hit her, did he hit them too? She decided if she was still alone when she finished with her shower, she would call there just to make sure they were alright.

After gingerly getting out of the shower and really getting a good look at her bruised and battered body, she slipped her robe on and left the bathroom. She looked out of the window and her father was not there, he was supposed to go and look at her car so she thought that is where he might have gone. She slowly walked to the phone and dialed Sammie's house.

Sammie: "Suzie, is that you? Are you okay? What happened last night?"

Suzie: "Yes, it's me. No, I'm not okay, you killed our son last night when you beat the hell out of me. Are the boys okay?"

Sammie: "What? Suzie I don't know what happened. I need to see you, can you get here?"

Suzie: "No, I wrecked my car last night to keep the boys from being taken away from you. I just wanted to make sure they were okay."

Sammie: "Yes, the boys are fine. What happened, I don't remember anything. Did you come here?"

Suzie: "Yes I was there. Sammie after you beat the hell out of me I lost our son, I can't talk right now."

She hung up the phone. The phone rang and she let it ring. When it stopped, she called Kim to tell her she had wrecked her car the night before. Kim was really upset and asked if she wanted her to come over. Suzie told her no, she was really not feeling well at all. Kim told her if she needed anything to call her and she promised she would. She then called Jean who was very upset. Suzie told her what she had done to the car and why. She started ranting that he should be in jail and those kids would be better off without him. Suzie got her to stop and told her she just wanted to try to figure out what she was going to do next. She told Jean that she was going to call in for the next week or so and work on her car if it could be fixed. Jean told her that her father had already called work and told them she would be out for at least a week. Jean let her know that if she needed anything she could call her. Suzie knew that and was grateful for both Kim and Jean.

She made her way back to her room as the phone started ringing again, she ignored it. She very gingerly dressed in shorts and an old top. She tried to brush her hair but her ribs hurt so badly she could not get her arm up to even do that. She heard her father come home and went down the hall to see him. He took one look at her and she could see he was not happy. All he said was, "Don't tell me that he did this to you." She shook her head no, it was from the accident, and her father just looked at her. He told her the car could be sort of fixed, it would never look the same and he had arranged to have it towed to the house. She knew he knew more than he was saying and then he told her, "If I ever catch you near Sammie again, I WILL have him arrested for statutory rape and you won't be able to stop me this time." She just shook her head, not wanting to argue.

Her father told her he had to go and do some things for a couple of hours, the car should be there soon and they would start working on it the next day. Today, she was to rest and he told her he had arranged to take the next week off from work so they could get her car running since college started soon, like she cared. Her father left. She didn't care about anything at all. She just kept thinking about Jonathan.

The phone kept ringing, almost every couple of minutes. Finally she couldn't take listening to it any longer and answered it knowing who would be on the other end.

Sammie: "Baby I am so sorry. I started drinking after I argued with the boys' mother and I don't even remember you coming here. What happened, please tell me."

Suzie: "Sammie, I really don't want to talk about it right now. I lost our son last night and I wrecked my car to keep you from losing your kids. If anyone knew what you had done to me, your ass would be in jail right now and God only knows where those kids would be."

Sammie: "I am so sorry baby, I wish I could just hold you right now."

Suzie: "Well, you can't because you also broke a couple of my ribs and my pelvis is cracked along with my face being bruised. You did this to me, you killed our son. It was a boy, Jonathan, he was so little, so precious and you killed him."

She couldn't take listening to his voice any longer so she hung up the phone. She knew Sammie was crying, she could hear it and she felt that he deserved to be crying. She just did not know what she was going to do, she was numb and dear God every inch of her hurt.

She tried laying down and it just hurt too much so she went out on the back deck and sat on the stairs. Like a movie the previous nights' events replayed themselves over and over in her mind. She cried almost the entire day. She heard the phone ring over and over again but would not and could not bring herself to even hear his voice again right now. She was 17 years old and felt like she had already lived a lifetime.

It was sometime later that she heard her father come home. The phone had stopped ringing and she was a little afraid that Sammie would come over. She knew if he did that and her father was here then all hell would break loose. She also knew that her father knew he had done something to her, she did not need that right now. She just did not want to see him anyway. How could someone who told her he loved her treat her like this? What did she know about this anyway, she was just a kid?"

She heard the truck bringing her car home. She went outside and when she saw it, she sat on the front stairs and just cried, she had done this to save his kids. If anything, those boys would not go to the state. It broke her heart, she loved her car and now it was a mess. Her father gently hugged her and said they could get it looking pretty good and get it back on the road. Maybe that would be good, they could do it together over the next week and it would keep her mind off of what had happened. She felt protected because she knew Sammie wouldn't call if he knew her father was home and he was the last person she wanted to talk to. She saw a glint down the road and glanced that way. Sammie had driven over to the house but stayed on the back road. She couldn't even bear to react in any way, she just went inside.

Chapter 34

With each day it got a little easier to move around. Her father had told her he knew something else had happened that night because she was too bruised from just the car accident. He told her again that if he caught her anywhere near him, his ass would be in jail. Suzie did not give any response to her father, she figured he did know more than he was saying but she also knew he didn't know she had lost her child. They worked hard on the car and it was starting to look decent, it would never be the same but she would be able to drive it. Drive it she thought, a constant memory of what had happened. She vowed she would finish Berkeley, get a good job and buy another car. She learned about doing body work on the car and it was fun to spend time with her father the way they used to. Betty had come up a couple of days and tried to help, she cooked dinners for them and she was always pleasant to be around. Suzie had also spoken with her mother. Of course, she was still on a rant about it being her fault and she was probably drinking. Suzie said nothing, if only she knew.

During the week, the swelling subsided, the bruises had started to fade to that sickly green color and Suzie looked awful. The pain in her pelvis had eased a bit, but the pain in her side was often excruciating; not to mention what she felt in her heart. She saw Kim but never told anyone what really had happened that night except for Jean. It was a secret heartache that she would keep to herself for many years. She knew she was going to have to face Sammie at some point, if anything she wanted an answer as to what the hell he was thinking that night. Not only was she hurt and confused, she was also getting angry. She had never been exposed to someone who drank like that and got violent but she had read about it. She always thought about the boys. What must they be thinking? All their plans, her ring, their dreams, gone; not to mention Jonathan, their son.

She wasn't sure if she could ever trust him again. How could she? Then while putting some finishing touches on the front of the car, she decided she needed to see him. She wanted to see what he had to say if anything, but more importantly she really wanted to see for herself that the boys were okay.

Between working on the car and getting ready to move, she was busy enough to not really think about much over the next week. She still hurt and hurt a lot, emotionally she was numb, and would she ever feel anything again? She doubted it. Her father took her to Columns one night for dinner after the bruises had faded enough for her to cover with the make-up she had at home. Of course, Stan was there. What was with this guy, she wondered why he didn't go places people his age hung out? This restaurant catered to old people. Stan talked to her and he asked her if she wanted to go out sometime. She told him not right now that there was too much going on but thanked him for asking.

He seemed quiet and mild mannered. Maybe after some time, she would take him up on his offer, but not right now. She still had much to sort out and certainly was far from trusting anyone, but she had to start doing something to keep her father at bay about Sammie. He only made a few comments now and then and they were not very nice.

Finally, the car was able to be driven and she felt like she could go back to work. Jean and Kim had kept in touch with her, and Sammie still called but she kept hanging up on him. She knew that she would have to talk to him sooner or later so she decided that the following Saturday night she would go over there after work. She knew that her father was going to be with Betty because the following weekend they were moving into the rental house. Ironic she thought, the weekend they were supposed to have their cookout and she was planning on facing the one person who had devastated her.

The days seemed normal enough, but every night she cried herself to sleep. Her baby, Jonathan, he was so sweet, so tiny. He had fit in the palm of her hand and his little hands were gathered into fists, he was so precious. She just couldn't seem to get that memory from her head. She did not know at the time that she never would. That memory would be something she carried in her heart and soul for the rest of her life. She also did not know that she had been having nightmares and was screaming. Her father heard her and was infuriated, but he had no proof Sammie had done something to her so he could not do anything. But God help him, if he ever caught her near that bastard again he would have him thrown in jail, kids or no kids. He never said anything to Suzie about the screaming he heard, but it worried him, he just did not know what had happened that night but he knew it was more than what she had told him.

She called Sammie on Friday and she told him that she was coming over after work on Saturday. She was not staying, she was coming to talk. He still wasn't sure what had happened. She had heard about people who drank so much that they blacked out, but she couldn't understand it because he did not drink or so she thought.

When she arrived at Sammie's he was pacing in the driveway. He ran to the car as she pulled in and she just put her hand up to stop him. She got out of the car moving slowly because her ribs and pelvis still hurt. He started toward her and she stopped him. She told him she would walk by herself. He tried to hand her the ring and she shook her head no. What did he think they could just go on after what he had done? He followed her up the stairs. She still had very light traces of bruising on her face and he could see them. He looked at her and just started crying.

Suzie: "I came over here tonight to make sure that the boys were okay."

Sammie: "They're fine, why?"

Suzie couldn't even answer him. She wanted to see the boys but they were either told to stay in their rooms or were not even there, she didn't know. She just sat on the sofa looking straight ahead, not even able to look at him.

Sammie: "Suzie, I have been beside myself worrying about you. I don't remember anything about that night. I just remember waking up when your father came here banging on the door looking for you, you weren't here and you were supposed to be. Please, tell me what happened."

Suzie: "I came over here after work. You weren't outside and the house was dark. I came up the stairs and you came out of the bedroom and punched me in the face. I fell down the stairs and you followed me. You kept hitting me and then you started kicking me. I went down the other stairs and you followed me. I couldn't get away from you. You kept kicking and hitting me. You finally stopped and I was able to get away from you to the car."

Sammie: "Oh, God, baby, I am so sorry. I have been going through hell trying to figure out what had happened to you. I had no idea. After your father came here I drove over to your house, saw the police and saw that you had had an accident. What happened?"

Sammie started crying and he reached for her hand but she pulled away from him. She told him about her ribs, pelvis, the bloody nose, lip and all the other bruises he had left on her. When he finally asked about the baby, she just started crying. She told him that he had kicked her in the stomach and caused her to lose the baby. He just hung his head, sobbing.

Sammie: "I must have blacked out. I don't remember anything. My God, I love you so much, I'd never hurt you or the baby on purpose. I don't know what I can say to you."

Suzie: There's nothing you can say, there's not much I can say either. The baby was a boy. He was so tiny. I held him, I held Jonathan and kissed him goodbye and all I could think is that you killed our son."

She couldn't take being around him any longer. Suzie got up to leave with tears streaming down her face. Sammie did not know what to say and neither did she. She just wanted to leave. He started to get up to stop her but the way she looked at him told him it was just better to let her go.

She left and went to the back of the lake. How could she even think about being with him again after what he had done to her, to their son? It just seemed that the last three years of her life had been hell, but nothing compared to what she was feeling at that moment. He made everything better in her life and now he had destroyed it. She sat there staring at the lake for a long time before she could even move. She just could not conceive that he did not know or remember what he had done to her that night.

The phone was ringing when she got home and she knew it was Sammie. She did not have any desire to talk to him then and wasn't sure she ever could again. She kept thinking that maybe if she were older she would know how to handle this better, but right now she had no clue. Drinking, she had never seen him drink, what the hell was going on. Is this what his mother meant by him being better now than he has been in a long time? She didn't know and she just wanted to sleep.

Chapter 35

Sleep, that night as had been, was difficult. The dreams that she was having were making her remember everything, almost as if she could still feel his fists and feet. She remembered seeing Jonathan and that was the most painful, she always woke up screaming. She retreated into a shell and just went through the motions of the things that were expected of her. Kim and Jean were very concerned about her, she kept trying to tell them that she was fine but Jean knew better, Kim did also but she still did not know the whole story.

Three days later, the phone rang after not ringing for a couple of days and she answered. It was Sammie's mom. She was crying and told her that there was no excuse for what he had done to her. She told her that her heart went out to both of them. Suzie was already crying and found it very difficult to talk. His mom seemed to understand and just kept talking. She asked Suzie if there would ever be any possibility of forgiving her son. Suzie started to get angry. Forgive him? Just how the hell could she even ask her to do that when he had killed their son? She told his mother that she needed time and wasn't really sure she could ever forgive him. She just didn't know.

His mom continued to tell her about his drinking problems and all the issues he had. Suzie had not been aware of the drinking problems but had an idea about all the other things his mother was sharing. She just asked her how she could love him if she didn't trust him. Suzie asked if the boys were okay and was told that they were but, missed her terribly, that she did not want to hear. It broke her heart. She didn't want to hear any more so she told his mom that she had to go and hung up the phone.

She wandered around the house that was now packed, she was numb and felt nothing. Jean had convinced her that she needed to see the doctor and that appointment was for the next day. She wasn't even sure what she would tell him. She didn't care, she didn't care about anything. She just kept wandering around aimlessly.

She worked the next morning and just went through the motions. It was pretty obvious to everyone that something was seriously wrong but she knew that Jean had told them to just leave her alone. Going to the doctor alone was another torture she had to endure. After telling him she lost the baby when she fell down the stairs, he did a thorough examination and found everything looked good. He sternly warned her to not attempt to get pregnant again for at least the next six months. He also told her that if anything like that ever happened again, she was to go to the hospital immediately because she could have ruptured her uterus. She knew that but she could not do that then. He told her to start taking the birth control pills again. Shit, she thought, what for, they didn't work the first time. She left his office feeling an emptiness that would find a place in her heart forever. Her son, their son was gone forever. She thought she had gone through hell when she was raped, well that couldn't even come close to what she was feeling now.

She met her father at Columns for dinner that night and Stan was there. She could have cared less. Seeing anyone was the furthest thing from her mind. He asked her to go to the movies one night and she said she would. She figured she better do something to act like things were normal, she certainly did not want to have to explain anything to her father, not now.

She knew Sammie had been checking up on her. She saw his car down the road from the house a couple of times and knew he was still calling but she couldn't bear to talk to him. She didn't know how she felt anymore, she didn't know anything. She thought back to the best part of what they were and she missed that terribly. Everything seemed like it was going to be perfect, the fairy tale ending that every girl dreams of. She caught herself looking at her bare finger and remembering her ring as she caught herself putting her hand on her stomach now and then remembering the tickle feeling she felt when Jonathan would move. He was gone. Jean tried to help with all of these feelings but she didn't even know what to tell her. Suzie knew that she was going to have to make some sort of decision and soon. Her heart broke for what they once had, where they were headed; would there ever be any way to recapture those times, she just didn't know.

For a couple of weeks Suzie let Stan take her to the movies and they met at Columns with her father and Betty. She tried to laugh and act like nothing was wrong but it was always forced. Her father knew that he was right about something being seriously wrong but he did not push the issue. She wasn't seeing Sammie and that made him happy. The move to the rental house went smoothly and school started so Suzie was at least occupied with other thoughts or at least she tried to be.

Stan was hanging around more and more. He kept trying to get her to have sex with him but she just couldn't bring herself to. She knew that he would never make her feel the way Sammie had. No one would ever make her feel like Sammie had because she vowed she would never let herself feel like that again. She started thinking that maybe she should talk to Sammie to see how she felt being around him. It had been a few weeks since she had seen him. Maybe she should just leave. She thought of going to her grandparents, they lived closer to the school than she did, but she knew she couldn't do that. Her mother had her convinced that they did not want anything to do with her since she had decided to stay with her father. God, that seemed like a lifetime ago when she made that decision. It had just been months.

School was okay, it was s diversion. The store was really good about working her hours around her schedule. Jean had observed that Suzie seemed a little more interested in doing make overs with her even though she really wasn't. She had to keep up this persona so everyone would stop asking her questions and leave her alone. When she arrived home after school on Friday, the phone was ringing. She didn't have much time, she had to go to work so she answered and it was Sammie. Hearing his voice destroyed her. This was hurting so much, she couldn't stand it. She did want to see him but she wasn't sure if she could or even should. The first thing he said was that he loved her. She told him that if he loved her, he wouldn't have hit her. He kept rambling on about how sorry he was and if there was any way she could ever consider forgiving him. He missed her, then he hit hard, he told her

195

the boys missed her. She missed them too, she loved those boys. She couldn't continue on the phone and told him she had to go to work.

She thought Jean was working that night but she wasn't. It was pretty obvious that she was extremely upset so they just let her straighten up the store. She was in the make-up aisle when she heard his voice. She turned around to find Sammie on his knees in the aisle crying, begging her to give him another chance or to at least talk about what happened. In her tormented mind she thought that he must love her if he was doing this. He followed her around on his knees for a while pleading with her. She told him that one day next weekend she would come to the house and they would talk. She really needed to either go back to him or end it forever. She looked up and saw Stan coming down the card aisle. She looked down at Sammie, he looked up and saw Stan. This was not going to be good.

She felt the hatred fill the air between them. Stan went out the back door and Sammie went out the front door. Stan came back with a 2X4 and Sammie came back with a tire iron, oh my God, what was happening? She wasn't sure if Stan had a temper or not but she knew Sammie did, if he was drinking but she didn't think he had been because she did not smell alcohol. The boss saw what was going on and came toward the scene. He pulled Suzie out of the way shoving a Valium in her mouth and told her he had called the police. What the hell was going on? The police, oh my God, this can't be, please don't let Sgt. Devane come this time.

The police came while Stan was standing there wielding the 2X4 and Sammie was just holding the tire iron, Suzie had become hysterical. The cop who walked the beat in town showed up. She would later learn that he was Stan's brother, what a mess. Suzie told Sammie she would be over Saturday night. She told Stan that she did not want to see him right now and to leave her alone for a while. The situation calmed down. Sammie left first and Suzie knew he was going to be following her for a while. How much more was she going to have to endure?

Chapter 36

Suzie went home after work and fixed herself one stiff drink. She was going to see Sammie again and all this was just too much for her. She decided to go to the Columns to see if her father was there. He was but so was Stan and she was grateful that he had not said anything to her father about what had occurred earlier. She ordered something to eat and had a couple more drinks. Thankfully, Stan left.

Suzie, her father and Betty talked about how the move had gone and what she was planning to do this weekend. She told them that she was going to work on her room and just relax on Sunday. Her father tried to inquire about what had happened with Sammie and she just said she did not want to talk about it. Her father then shared that he really did like Sammie, he seemed like a really nice guy, but he just felt that he was too old her for and she had her whole life ahead of her. That was quite a revelation and she wondered what her father would think if he knew what had really happened.

During the next few days between school, work and doing things with Kim, she was busy and the days went quickly. Nothing made sense to her either. She couldn't fathom that someone would not remember what they had done. She talked with one of the pharmacists about blacking out from drinking. He told her that it was quite possible if a person had a serious drinking problem, hadn't drank in a while and then drank a lot. She understood, but still could not get the concept that Sammie had a problem with alcohol.

Her father had told her that he was going to be with Betty that weekend so he was gone when she arrived home. She knew she was still having nightmares but her father had stopped asking about them. She knew she would dream again that night because her visit to Sammie's was on her mind. Maybe he could answer some of these questions tomorrow. She cried herself to sleep that night as she had many nights previously and would continue to do so for a long time to come.

Saturday came, it was a beautiful day, getting close to the end of September. She should have been living with Sammie and getting ready to have their baby. Those thoughts made her cry as she showered. She knew she needed to calm down, but she couldn't. Would she ever be able to forget?

She arrived at Sammie's and he was in the driveway pacing frantically. She could tell immediately that he was very nervous, unsettled. When she saw him her heart ached for the way things had once been and she wasn't sure how she felt about him. Could they ever recapture what once was? The only way to find out was to face all this and face him. He started to move toward her and she stopped him. The last thing she wanted was for him to touch her right then. She got out of the car and went upstairs.

The house was quiet and she wanted to know where the boys were. Sammie shared that he had taken them to his mother's. Since his mother really wanted them to get back together she was glad to take them. Suzie was a little disappointed since she had not seen them prior to that night but it was for the best, they needed to talk. She asked Sammie if they were okay and he told her that they were missing her and not happy that she wasn't around. This broke her heart because she really did love them.

Sammie let Suzie lead the way and she sat on the sofa in the corner. He started to sit next to her but thought better of it and moved to the other side. He had to move slowly, very slowly if he ever stood a chance of getting her back. He had been missing her terribly and his heart was shattered with what he had done, not just to their son but to her. He wasn't sure he could even go on without her. She just didn't know what or how to feel. She realized that her hand was on her stomach and she saw that he noticed also. She looked at him and he was crying, she moved her hand.

Sammie: "Suzie, I just don't know what to say to you. Telling you I'm sorry just doesn't seem to be enough. I just don't know what happened. All I know is that I had been so worried about talking to your father because he certainly had it in his power to forever keep us apart, I have also been so worried about you having been so sick, and I was also missing Cara and Jack. I called my ex and we had a horrible fight. All I remember is having a drink. I don't' remember anything else until your father was pounding on the front door asking if you were here. It was very late and I told him that you were not here. He kept yelling that you had disappeared and he couldn't find you. I was beside myself because I didn't know anything that had happened. I went looking for you and saw the accident. I didn't know what to think because I couldn't go to you right then. All I do know is that I love you more than anything or anyone in this world and I really want to fix us."

Suzie: "I'm not sure we can fix this. You not only hurt me physically, you killed our baby, our son. How do I ever look at you and not remember what you did to me. Emotionally, I'm a wreck. I don't care about anything or anyone anymore. I don't even know how I feel about you right now."

Sammie: "I do understand, I really do and I deserve all the horrible feelings you are having. Can you please tell me about that night?"

Chapter 37

Suzie sat very quietly for a few moments processing all he had said to her. Her thought was to make him hurt as much as she was hurting. She realized that he was devastated by what had happened. He wanted to know everything, well fine, she was going to tell him. Through her tears and a choked voice she began.

She told him everything but went into more detail about what had happened when she lost Jonathan. She told him what he looked like and how tiny he was. This was more difficult than she thought it was going to be and she wasn't sure she could finish. He sat listening to her just staring ahead with his hands folded together. When she talked about Jonathan she noticed that his hands clenched together so tightly that his knuckles were white. She had to stop, she couldn't go on.

Sammie rose and started pacing the living room as was his habit when he was disturbed about something. He was crying, the tears flowing freely. He had hurt her and it was pretty obvious that she was hurting him now but it didn't feel good. She collapsed in a heap, holding her face in her hands and crying uncontrollably. She knew she was hurting him terribly and this was just not her, she did not like hurting anyone and it was like a knife in her heart. She wondered if she still cared for him. She was sure that she did on some level but how could she ever trust him again? She got up and went to the rest room. She could hear him continue to pace.

While in the rest room, she washed her face with cold water. Her makeup had streaked down her face, she washed it off. Her face was blotchy, her eyes were swollen and there were still faint traces of bruises on her face.

Returning to the living room Sammie had taken a seat on the sofa again. He was slumped over with his head in his hands. He looked up when he heard her return, his eyes were swollen and tears continued to run down his face. He saw her face and showed the horror he felt.

> Sammie: "I want to hold you so badly. I am horrified at what I have done, just horrified. I would never intentionally hurt you and our son, my God, I can't believe I have done this to us."

Suzie just looked at him and sat back down on the opposite side of the sofa, she still wasn't sure she even wanted to be close to him. She could see the hurt in his eyes and it bothered her. She continued with the story of how she wrecked her car to keep her father from knowing what he had done to her although she knew her father knew more than he was saying. She also emphasized that she did that more for the boys so they wouldn't be taken away from him if the police go involved and he went to jail.

> Suzie: "Trust me, at that moment in time, you could have gone to prison and I wouldn't have cared. But those boys had nothing to do with what happened and they've had enough problems in their young lives, they didn't need that to happen to them"

When she spoke those words it hit him just how vile she had been. God, he wasn't sure that he could do anything to make things better. He knew that he could never make this up to her but he still loved her, loved her more than anything in the world. He wasn't sure she would ever believe that again let alone trust him.

When Suzie finished the story she just curled up on the sofa and continued to cry, she could hear Sammie crying also. She still was not sure how she felt about him. In some remote part of her heart, she knew she still loved him beyond anything she ever knew but would she ever be able to trust him again. She just wasn't sure.

She felt Sammie move, he moved a bit closer to her and she did not react. After all of this hurt and what he had done, she really did want to be in his arms again. She wanted to feel safe, secure, protected and she wanted him to take away all this pain. How could she think that, protected in the arms of the man who destroyed her, them? She just didn't know what to think.

Suddenly she felt his hand on her shoulder and that caused her to jump. When she looked at Sammie, she knew he was devastated that he had that effect on her. She felt that she had succeeded in destroying him, but it didn't feel good. She reached her hand over and placed it over his, it was the first move she had made toward him at all. He wasn't sure how to deal with that.

He very quietly started talking through a choked voice of his own.

Sammie: "After your father came to the house that night, I sobered up pretty quickly. Honestly baby, I had no recollection of you coming here and I didn't know where the boys were either. After your father left, I left and drove to your house. I had to find out what was going on, I didn't know where you were, if you were okay, if the baby was okay. As I drove down the street to your house, I saw your father and Sgt. Devane standing in the road but I didn't see you. The tow truck was pulling your car from the woods. I didn't know where you were, all I thought is that you had either been taken to the hospital or were dead. I was scared to death. I didn't know what to do, but then you walked up the hill a little bit and I could see you. I also saw that you had blood on your face and down your dress. I wanted to go to you but I knew I couldn't with your father and the police there. I didn't know what to think so I just went home. I didn't sleep for a couple of days after you initially told me what happened. I kept trying to call you but you either wouldn't answer or kept hanging up, now I know why. I talked to my mother and she is beyond furious with me."

Sammie had been crying while he told her all of this, but he was crying even harder now. Suzie listened and when she found out he had called his mother she was even more furious. Then she thought she shouldn't be because she had turned to Jean. But, she knew one thing, his mother was not the only one who was furious with him. She kept hearing his mother's voice telling her that she had been the best thing that had happened to him in a long time and he's been so much better since meeting her. Now she wondered what his worst was. Suzie remained silent.

Sammie: "Suzie, I stopped drinking when I met you. I have had an issue with alcohol for some time. I have been so upset that we couldn't be together through the entire early stages of the pregnancy, you had been so sick, not eating or sleeping. I've also been really worried about telling your father because I don't think he would have reacted well at all and I can't go to jail. Then dealing with missing Cara and Jack just made everything so much worse. When I argued with the ex that was the last straw. I am so sorry, I don't think you will ever know how sorry I am. The only thing I am sure of at this moment is that I love you more than you know, more than I even knew."

Sammie sat there crying with his head resting in his hands. He was hurting more than she even thought was possible. Suzie got up and went to the phone in the kitchen, dialed her boss's number and told him that she was not feeling well. She would not be in to work the next morning. Sammie wasn't sure what to make of this, but he said nothing as she returned to the sofa and curled back up into a ball. He could not stand what he had done to her, their son and to them. He loved her so much and he was furious with himself.

Finally, after what seemed like an eternity, she looked up at him.

Suzie: "Sammie, I honestly don't know if I can ever trust you would never do that to me again. I was raised in a family where it is just not acceptable for a man to hit a woman. You told me a long time ago that you would never do anything to hurt me and now you have destroyed me, everything that we had and you killed our son. My pelvis hurts, my ribs hurt whenever I move, not to mention that you have broken my heart. I just don't know what to do, but I do know that somewhere deep inside I still love you. Why? I don't know but I do, and the boys, my God I so love them. I don't know if we can ever get back to where we were. I just know that right now I want to stop hurting."

Sammie slowly moved to the coffee table in front of her. He was still crying but he took her hands and sat there holding them for several minutes because he was just too choked up to speak.

Suzie: "Did you ever hit a woman before? You don't hit the boys do you? Did your father hit your mother?"

Sammie: "Yes, I did hit my ex-wife once. I haven't raised a hand to the boys except once or twice since I met you. Yes, my father did hit my mother. I hated it and I hate what I have done to you because I had promised you I would never hurt you. It hurts so much to know that you find it difficult for me to even hold your hands, but I do understand. I can't promise that I will never hurt you again because we are going to hurt each other now and then, but I do promise that I will never touch another drop of alcohol again and I will never hit you again."

Suzie: "How can you even promise that, you don't know what the future holds? What happens the next time you argue with your ex?

You argue with her and I get beat. I just don't know if I can trust you again.

Sammie: "I deserve that. What if we take things very slowly and just see how it works out. I doubt we will get back to where we were any time soon, but Suzie, I love you so much and I want to try. I can't bear the thought of losing you."

Suzie: "I don't know. I really need to think about this Sammie. I'm tired, my body still hurts and losing Jonathan has just left me feeling dead inside. I know physically I will heal with time, but I don't know if emotionally I ever will. I don't even know if I can let you touch me again. I just don't know."

With that, Suzie curled back up in a ball and closed her eyes, she didn't want to say anything else or talk to him any further right now. She felt Sammie move to the sofa next to her, not too close, but she could feel the heat from his body. He gently put his arm around her and pulled her to him so she would be more comfortable. She let him do this, she just did not have any more fight left in her. She wanted to sleep, a night without the nightmare. She leaned against him and fell asleep.

She did not feel him pick her up from the sofa and lay her on the bed. He stood in the doorway watching her sleep, as tears filled his eyes and he wondered how in the hell he could have ever hurt this sweet, beautiful young woman the way he did. He loved her for God's sake. He hated himself for what he had done and made a feeble promise to never make her feel unsafe again. He went to the sofa to just lay down, he was exhausted but did not want to rouse her by laying down next to her. He had not slept well since that night. Laying there staring at the ceiling, the tears flowed endlessly as he wondered if there would be anything he could ever do to make this up to her? He decided to take things very slowly and let her lead the way. He convinced himself he would have to have patience, but this was something he wanted more than anything in this world and he would do whatever it took to regain her trust.

Just as his eyes closed, he heard the blood curdling scream. He jumped from the sofa and couldn't get to the bedroom fast enough. She was having a nightmare. Oh God, what was she dreaming about? He went to her and sat next to her on the bed. She was now moaning and calling out for the baby. He gently placed his hands on her shoulders but she did not wake. He started to pull her to him so he could hold her. She woke up and started fighting him.

Sammie: "Shhh sweetheart, I'm here, you're okay. It was a nightmare. I've got you."

She allowed herself to settle into his arms, crying on his shoulder, he just held her and rubbed her back gently. He wanted to ask what the nightmare was about, he didn't have to, he knew. Convinced that she had been doing this since that night made his heart ache even more. He wished he could take these nightmares from her. She finally settled down and he slid onto the bed next to her so he could hold her. She didn't fight him, she just fell back asleep.

He did not sleep at all, he just wanted to keep her safe. He felt her move and as she roused realizing where she was, she jumped up and away from his grasp with her heart racing. He looked at her and told her that she had a nightmare, screamed and he was just holding her. He wanted to share this horror which he had caused her. She just stood there staring down at him trying to calm down. This was going to take a long time and he was ready for whatever he needed to do. Without saying a word, she went to the restroom. God, what had he done to her?

Chapter 38

He went to the kitchen to fix them something to eat. That was something he knew she had not been doing either because she had lost quite a bit of weight. She went to the kitchen when she smelled the food. Initially it turned her stomach but she remembered how much she enjoyed the breakfasts he used to make for her. Sitting down to watch him, she decided that she needed to eat. Maybe after some food and coffee she would feel like talking some more. There was still a lot she had left unsaid.

They ate in silence at the dining room table. It was not often that they ate there but that is where he went to sit and she just followed him. Sammie just hated the way things were, they used to be so close and this was torturous. They finished eating and he cleaned up the dishes. He found her standing by the stereo looking out of the window. She had set the stereo up to play but had not turned it on. She felt him behind her and turned to look him directly in the eye.

Suzie: "Sammie, for the life of me I don't know why I am going to say what I have to say but this is what I have been thinking about."

Sammie: "I'm listening."

Suzie: "I know you were holding me last night after the nightmare. Every time I dream it is the same thing. I see your fists and feet coming at me and then the nurse is taking Jonathan away from me. I have never in my short life felt so empty, alone, or scared. It helped having you hold me. It helped to know you were going through it with me even if you didn't know what it was about at the time. I don't know if I can ever really sleep again."

Sammie: "You will. You can stay here any time you want and I will just hold you for as long as you want me to. I don't ever want to let you go."

Suzie: "I can't stay tonight because I have to go to school in the morning and my father should be home. He knows something really bad happened that night because he is convinced that all of my bruises were not from the accident alone. I don't know how often I can get here and for the life of me I don't know why but I want to be here. I just need to know that you will not push me to do anything I'm not ready for."

Sammie: "I will not push you at all, you tell me what you want and when you want it. I'll tell the boys that since the car accident you have not been feeling well, which is the truth and you need time to heal. They will understand. They have missed you so much and I know you have missed them. Not to mention how much I have missed you."

Suzie: "Good, just let it be for right now. I won't be able to get over here at all this week which will be hell because Jean and now you are the only two who know what really happened that night. We just need to take this very slowly because honestly it is going to take me a long time to trust you again, if I ever can."

Sammie: "I understand, just remember that I love you more than anything in the world."

She took a small step forward but lowered her head. He gently folded her in his arms and held her. She felt tired again and wanted to lay down so she went to the bedroom and did just that. He went with her and just held her as he said he would do. When he knew she was asleep, he slipped out of the room, went to the living room and just cried. He was still having great difficulty trying to remember what he had done to her, then he thought about Jonathan and cried even harder. He had killed his son, would he ever be able to get over what he had done? Would this only serve to destroy them completely?

He dozed off sobbing. Hearing her screams, he ran to her and held her tight. She was hysterical and shaking. He tried to soothe her by rubbing her back and whispering gently to her. What in God's name did she do when she was by herself? How was she explaining these nightmares? He was sure that her father must have heard her when she screamed.

She fell into a fitful sleep and he stayed right there with her. It was beginning to scare him that she was falling into a depression she would not come out of. He was worried and decided that he was going to have to watch her more closely even if it were from afar.

208

Chapter 39

The next week was very difficult for both of them. They knew that they would see each other that coming weekend and it couldn't get there fast enough for either of them. During the week Suzie had met her father at Columns after work almost every night for dinner. It was nice to not have to cook. Her father was worrying about her since she still was not herself. Stan was there one night and he tried to talk to her. She simply told him that she still wasn't really feeling up to seeing anyone and left things at that.

She did have fleeting thoughts about him while driving home that night. He was quiet and soft spoken, but she shook her head still very confused about what she was even thinking. She knew that in some remote corner of her heart, she still loved Sammie but wasn't sure if she could stay with him. Maybe she would have a better idea after this weekend how she felt which would guide her a bit more. She honestly did not know and really didn't care.

Between work and school, the week went relatively quickly. Suzie remained quiet and distant, she just wasn't interested in anything and laughing was something she just couldn't imagine ever doing again. Kim was good and their conversations were concentrated on wedding plans, although Kim knew something was going on. Suzie just assured her that she was still upset about wrecking her car and that she and Sammie were having some problems right now, nothing she wanted to talk about. Kim had to believe her friend, but she knew there was more to this than what she was saying. Suzie really wanted the next few months to go by so she could graduate from Berkeley and find a good job so she could just leave all this behind her. She didn't know what she was going to do and really didn't care.

She had asked for the weekend off and they were very accommodating at work. Jean was still really worried about her since she had shown no further interest in doing make overs. Jean did not want her to see Sammie again but she wasn't going to tell her that because Suzie needed someone she could trust to confide in and Jean would continue to keep an eye on her.

She had called Sammie one evening before she went to dinner and told him she would be there that Friday night. She knew him well enough to know that he would be looking forward to seeing her. She told her father that she was going to be at Kim's working on the wedding plans because Gary was away that weekend. Her father acted as if he believed her but she still didn't really care.

She arrived at Sammie's to find his car in the driveway, the garage door open and Sammie in the garage waiting for her. She pulled in and got out of the car as he closed the garage door. He wanted to give her the ring, carry her upstairs, just be normal, but he refrained. He promised her that he would take things slowly and he let her lead the way.

She went upstairs and the boys were really glad to see her and she them. They told her that their father had said once she got there they were going to go and get dinner, they wanted to know what she wanted. It was very difficult acting as if nothing was wrong, but she had to try. She told them that A&W would be fine because she knew they liked that. While they were talking, Sammie had brought her bag up to the bedroom which was fine. He asked Teddy if he wanted to stay with Suzie while they went to get the food and that was great with him.

Suzie knew that he had talked to the kids because they had refrained from asking any questions. Teddy was more concerned about the Mustang and would he be able to ride in it again. That was the only thing either of them asked and when she told Teddy he could someday, he smiled. He sat with her on the sofa and finally asked if she was okay. She assured him that she was and then heard his father returning. They ate in the living room. Suzie picked at her food managing to eat about half of it. Sam told her he was glad she wasn't getting sick anymore and that almost catapulted her into a flood of tears but she managed to control the urge. She knew he had no idea what had gone on.

After the boys went to bed, Sammie and Suzie talked. For a change, she sat on the coffee table but he could tell by her expression that this was going to be serious.

Suzie: "Sammie, I'm finding it very difficult right now to tell you that I love you. I still have very strong feelings for you, it's just hard to get the words out. I have no idea how I can even feel that way, but I do. I want to try and see where we can go to get us back together again. It's going to take a long time and I can't promise anything."

Sammie: "Oh baby, you have no idea how much I wanted to hear those words. We will take this one step at a time, slowly and if you want me to do anything, you will have to tell me because I'm not doing anything until you say so. I promise that."

Suzie: "Well, all I want to do is sleep tonight. I haven't slept well all week and I am really tired. I'm glad the boys were here, I missed them more than I even thought I had. I really do love those two."

Sammie: "I do too, they are good kids and they are being really good with you. I talked to them and told them what happened with the car but have not told them anything else."

Suzie feebly smiled, moved to the sofa and let Sammie hold her. She had her eyes closed as he rubbed her arm and wondered to herself if they could really get through all of this. She just didn't know. Do you stop loving someone? She was just so confused. She decided to just let things happen and see where it went. Something would tell her in time what would be the right thing to do.

All that night Sammie just held her so she could sleep. He would drift off but if she moved at all, he was wide awake. She had a very restless period early in the morning, but she did not scream or thrash around as she had done previously. He was just very happy to have her there and in his arms where he felt she belonged. He wanted to make love to her but had promised to follow her lead and refrained, that time would come.

She woke the following morning needing the restroom and could hear the boys up. She slipped gingerly from Sammie's grip and slipped out of the bedroom. Before she closed the door, she heard him snoring a little bit and couldn't help but smile. After she used the restroom she went to the kitchen and found the boys trying to figure out how to make pancakes. This brought a smile to her face, leave it to those two, she thought.

The three of them made breakfast together but it was a bit unsettling to Suzie. It just didn't seem to be as comfortable as it once was. She just couldn't get her heart into the activities and found herself constantly thinking about Jonathan. She wondered if that would ever stop. She would learn as the years went on that it wouldn't, she would just learn to live with that loss. She told the boys to wake their father so they could eat, they did that rather noisily and again, she smiled. Could she really do this? She wasn't sure.

They spent a quiet day together playing games with the boys and it was good. Sammie had not been to the grocery store so she sent him for some things so they could cook dinner. She needed to keep busy. He left with both of the boys which gave her a few minutes to herself. She would stare at the stairs and could feel each blow he dealt. Is this what it was going to be like from now on? Would it help if they bought a different house?

She went to the stereo and put on some of her Elvis Presley albums. She had the music loud when they returned and she went to prepare their dinner. She was making hamburgers and French fries. The boys were glad to help her and Sammie set the table but the atmosphere was nothing like it used to be. It all should have been so normal and natural but with every move she made, she realized she was forcing herself to do this.

After dinner the boys went to their friends down the street which gave Sammie and Suzie time alone. Sammie asked if she wanted her ring and she shook her head no. He told her that he would leave it where it was until she was ready. When they went to Vegas he would buy her another ring, a new ring for a new beginning. She had not thought that far ahead. She was not sure that she wanted to do that any longer, she was not sure about anything. She just shook her head. She did tell him she wanted to make love to him that night, she wanted to feel normal again. She had gone back on the pill and the doctor said these new ones should work.

Even though he wanted to make that night very special, he couldn't because the boys were home. They would have to quietly enjoy their night together in the bedroom. The boys returned home on time as they normally did. Suzie took a shower and went to the bedroom to wait for Sammie. She looked down at the drawer that contained all those beautiful negligees he had purchased for her but she just didn't have the heart to use any of them at the moment.

Sammie came in, closed the door and turned on the radio he had brought into the room. It wasn't very loud but it was enough to keep the boys from hearing them. Sammie was extremely gentle with her but she just couldn't get to the point of feeling anything, he tried and she faked it. They had made love enough for her to know she could do that. She also knew that he would know, but her heart wasn't really in it. It just didn't feel right any longer. Was this the answer she was looking for?

Sammie knew this was going to take some time and he was trying so hard to be patient. Everything had been so perfect between them and now it was so distant. He wondered himself if they would ever be able to recapture what they once had. Suzie fell asleep first and he held her for dear life. She was slipping away and he didn't know if he could hang on to her. This saddened him and he found sleep impossible.

She slept fairly well until very early in the morning. Sammie had slipped from the room for just a minute to use the restroom when he heard the blood curdling screams. He ran back to the bedroom and found her thrashing around, screaming and crying hysterically. He gently woke her and held her. The boys woke and wanted to know what that noise was. Sammie told them that she had a nightmare and that seemed to appease them. How could he have ever hurt this beautiful angel the way he had? He knew he was going to pay dearly for that mistake.

Suzie did not want to stay the entire day. She wanted to get away. She told them she had some homework to do and to get ready for the following week. The boys were disappointed and disappeared. Sammie told her that he understood but it felt as if she were leaving for good. His heart was broken but he just said he understood. She left.

Chapter 40

The next couple of weeks were busy. Suzie talked to Sammie but with the exception of him stopping in at the store, she did not see much of him. He just had to know that she was okay or at least appeared to be. A few of those times she had not even seen him, he wanted it that way. His heart was breaking as he knew hers was and he just wished she would turn to him to try to work this out together. He also knew he couldn't force himself into her life or to make her make a choice she wasn't ready to make. He had to have patience.

Suzie had met her father at Columns for dinner several nights during that time and Stan was always there. She found herself thinking more and more about Stan because the hurt she was experiencing just seemed intolerable. Every time she even thought about Sammie at all she thought about was how his fists and feet felt. She could not shake those images. Not to even mention Jonathan. Too much for a young girl to have to deal with. The other problem was she also could not imagine living without Sammie. She did allow Stan to take her to the movies only to keep her father from constantly asking questions or bugging her about going out.

Suzie looked at Stan as more of friend then a possible boyfriend, she really did not like him all that much. However, she did see him a couple of times and he also had come over to the house a few times. This seemed to make her father happy and when they were all sitting around talking, it did get her mind off of Jonathan for a few short minutes.

Sammie had called her and told her that he wanted to see her. She wanted to see him also because she had honestly been missing him. She couldn't understand why but she was. They managed to spend a couple of nights together but things were not getting any better. Not for lack of trying, but Suzie was having a great deal of difficulty even letting Sammie touch her. She still cried for what they had lost and even told Sammie that she would give anything to go back to the way things once were. He tried and his patience was amazing but it was still as if an ocean separated them.

She had gone out with Stan one evening and when he brought her home, her father was not there. She invited Stan in since he had been there previously. One thing led to another and even though Suzie did not really want to, they had sex. It certainly was nothing compared to the way it had been with Sammie. Actually, she really didn't care, she had lost her heart and soul to the memory of her son and what Sammie had done to her. She was still numb. Seeing both of them was not a good idea either and Suzie knew this even though it had only been a couple of weeks, it just wasn't right she needed to make some kind of decision.

Her confusion escalated as Sammie kept telling her that he wanted to see more of her. She understood that and she did spend more nights with Sammie which only proved to add to her confusion. The last weekend of October was a weekend getaway through Berkeley to a Dude Ranch. Kim and Suzie planned on attending this event. Kim thought it would be good for Suzie and Suzie felt it might be a good time to come to some kind of decision. She had to either show more interest in repairing this relationship with Sammie, and with Stan there really was no decision, she simply wasn't that interested. Prior to the weekend away, Suzie spent a couple nights with Sammie and it was just not right. Every time he even moved she found herself putting her hands up as if in defense of a blow. This was only proving to further break her heart and his also.

At the Dude Ranch, she was able to take one of the horses and ride through the fields. The ranch hands had seen that she was an accomplished rider so they let her go. She raced across the open field with the sun on her face and the wind in her hair and it was exhilarating. She stopped at the far end of the field and dismounted the horse. Sitting under a tree she started to think if she really wanted to try to put her and Sammie back together with this cavern of heartache between them. After all, he was pretty much old enough to be her father, he had four kids and he had hurt her more than she could have ever imagined. Then there was Stan, older than her, but younger with no kids and it would be like starting fresh. Even if it wasn't Stan she would have a fresh start and make her own memories with someone who didn't have memories either. But, she loved Sam and Teddy so much and knew it would break her heart to not see them again. Oh God, what should she do?

That night she called Sammie and Stan. Stan was a little more casual but they did not have a history to speak of, they would be making their own. Sammie was intense and she knew he was going to start getting impatient even though he had promised he wouldn't. He had told her that they could sell that house, get another one without the horrible memories but would that be enough to erase what he had done? What about their son? The first thing she thought of was his fist when she thought of Sammie. Then there was Jonathan, she had felt him move, felt his life, held his lifeless body, would those memories ever be tolerable? Sammie knew her very well, he could read her, her moods and they had grown to be able to finish each other's sentences, but was that enough? She did not doubt that Sammie loved her but how can you hurt someone you say you love? She found her hand rubbing her cheek and remembering the pain from his fist not to mention the rest of the blows she endured. With an extremely heavy heart and as hard as it was going to be, she was going to have to walk away. Then it hit her, if she walked away from Sammie, she would also be walking away from the two boys who she had come to love. She couldn't stay just because of them but it was going to be excruciatingly difficult to say goodbye.

The weekend ended and she knew she was going to have to confront Sammie. She still couldn't bring herself to do so and she spent a few more nights with him. She had told herself that she was reaching the depths to make sure she was making the correct decision. The middle of November she decided that was enough, she could no longer endure all the memories she faced when she walked into the house or even when she was around him. She had to tell him. She wasn't sure how he would react and that scared her. She did not want a repeat of that fateful night. She arrived at the house and the boys were nowhere in sight. Sammie knew that something was weighing very heavily on her mind and he asked about it. She simply told him she needed to talk to him.

With a very choked voice she told him and he started crying. He did not take the news very well. He tried to tell her that he would never hit her again, he would never drink again. He simply could not imagine his life without her in it. Then he tried to use the boys to keep her there. He began to raise his voice and that was pretty much what sealed her decision. She understood he was upset, she was also, she knew she still loved him but after what he had done to her how could she trust him again. If you can't trust someone, you can't respect them, if you can't respect them, you can't love them. Even though she knew in the deepest recesses of her heart that she did love him and always would. She wanted to say goodbye to the boys but they weren't there and she knew if she walked out of the door she would never see them again. She couldn't help it, she couldn't find it in herself to stay. She collected the albums she had brought there, left him crying and only prayed that he would never drink again.

She drove home with tears running down her face, a heavy heart and the memory of him and their brief life together tucked safely in her soul for the rest of her life. Suzie started seeing Stan more frequently mostly because he was just there and she had no ambition to 'date'. With all the time he was around her he never so much as ever raised his voice to her. Even if she didn't stay with him, he was good to have around when her father decided to stay with Betty and Suzie did not particularly like staying in this house alone. Besides, the holidays were just weeks away and she did not want to spend them alone.

She knew she was going to miss Sammie, but did not really know how much. Stan did not have the same finesse that Sammie had but Suzie just didn't care. She was still numb from everything she had been through for the last year and a half, she was just going through the motions. She made her decision and would have to learn to live with that and without Sammie.

Chapter 41

Suzie went to play one of the albums she had taken from Sammie's house the last day she was there. She discovered that all of the records in the sleeves had been switched for different records. This infuriated her and she decided that she would go to the house the next day and switch them around. She also decided that she wanted her ring, it was hers after all.

She knew the boys were in school and Sammie should be at work and her car in the driveway was nothing unusual. She would just go in and get the albums, her ring and leave. She wanted a piece of him and the good memories to hold on to forever but, was that all she wanted? In her tormented mind was she hoping that he would magically appear and make everything perfect again? Maybe, maybe not, she didn't know but she had a mission. She used the hidden key to let herself in since she had long since given Sammie back the key he had given her. She immediately went to where her ring was. It was still there and tucked inside the box was the ring and a folded up piece of paper. Suzie read it several times and cried. She really did not want things to end this way or at all actually but she just couldn't get past what he had done to her and their son. Her heart was torn to shreds as she read the words....

"We had a dream to become a team. We wished on the stars and heaven was almost ours. Before it could begin, fate stepped in to end it all. If it's true that this is goodbye, it will forever sadden me that we almost made it all the way. Suzie, I love you."

She left the piece of paper on his dresser and slipped the ring into her pocket. She went to the living room with a broken heart to switch the records. She heard a noise and turned around. Sammie was coming up the stairs. Oh shit, how did he know she was going to be there? He had his hand behind his back and she froze. All she could think was that he was going to start hitting her again. He walked up to her and took his hand from behind his back and he had a gun. He looked her straight in the eye as he brought the gun up and said, "If I can't have you then nobody can." With that he shot the gun but intentionally missed. He was too close to have missed. Suzie froze in complete shock.

He dropped the gun and sank to his knees crying hysterically. Suzie was frozen where she stood. Was he serious? Her ears were ringing and she started crying, what had he just done? She slowly let her glance move toward him. He was holding his head in his hands and crying. He finally looked up and told her that he did not want her to go, he could not imagine living his life without her. He started begging and begging her to stay saying over and over how sorry he was.

The banging of the door opening brought her out of her shock. She looked toward the stairs and the police were running up the stairs with their guns drawn. Sgt. Devane in the lead. When he saw the gun on the floor he motioned for the others to put their weapons away. Two of the officers grabbed Sammie and restrained him on the floor. Sgt. Devane took Suzie into the kitchen where he kept asking over and over what had happened.

Finally composing herself, she told him exactly what had happened, she just wanted her stuff, and he was supposed to be at work. She heard them getting Sammie off of the floor, sitting him down on the sofa and Suzie became hysterical. She did not want them to arrest him, he had the boys to take care of and there was no one else around to take them. Sgt. Devane told her that this was a serious offense. She knew that but begged him to not arrest him. She kept telling him over and over that she had just gone there for her stuff, he should have been at work. She told him that she was not seeing him any longer and it was over. Finally after some time, Sgt. Devane said they would not arrest him. He then helped Suzie get the rest of her things and he told her he was going to escort her home.

She looked one last time at Sammie as she moved through the living room. He was sitting on the sofa surrounded by the police. He looked so lost, he was crying and he looked up at her and mouthed, "I love you". She walked down the stairs with Sgt. Devane following her. As she reached the door she heard Sammie wail her name, "Suzie". She would never forget the sound of his voice. She got in the car and drove home with Sgt. Devane right behind her.

When they arrived, they stood outside talking for quite a while. He asked if she was serious about not seeing him and she said yes. After what he had done, how could she ever think of going back there? He then proceeded to tell her about the issues he was aware of with his drinking and driving issues. He had a very serious drinking history and Suzie was positive that Sgt. Devane had not told her the whole story. She really did not want to hear any more about how bad he was. All she told Sgt. Devane was he had his kids to take care of. Then a horrible thought hit her, did he hit the kids. Sgt. Devane told her that they had never been called to the house for any other reason than her and Sammie fighting and today. Although his arrest for drinking and driving was within the last two years. That made her feel better, she just could not imagine anyone hurting those boys. The boys, she would never see them again, that was almost as painful as losing Jonathan.

Chapter 42

The boys, it broke her heart to know she was never going to see them again. Sad for her and sad for them. She had no idea what he would tell them but she knew she was always going to miss them and think about them.

Suzie was in such a state of shock and depression, she just sank into an attitude of not caring about anything. As far as anyone was concerned she had chosen to leave Sammie because she wanted a new start, she wanted her own family and she thought it best to be with someone younger. She continued to see Stan. He was okay, she stopped comparing him to Sammie, she was just grateful for the peace. Her plan was to finish Berkeley and move somewhere where she could put all of this behind her and start a new life.

The next couple of weeks were difficult, not being able to see Sammie. He did not stop in the store again and she avoided where he worked. She was emphatically told that if they were ever seen together again, he would be going to jail. She couldn't risk that because of the boys. She missed them a lot but buried all of those feelings into her own private hell with the memories of Jonathan.

Just two weeks before Christmas that year, her father told her that when she turned 18 she was going to have to go out of her own because he was planning on moving in with Betty and there wasn't enough room for her there. What? Why? She would only have three more months of Berkeley left at that time and would be done, why couldn't he just wait a bit. On top of all that had been piled on Suzie, she discovered that she was once again pregnant. Oh my God, what was she going to do now and for just a little while she wondered......

Stan was taken back by this news. They talked about getting married and with what her father had told her it seemed like this was the solution to her situation. Honestly, she just didn't care anymore. She knew that she really didn't love Stan, maybe she would learn to love him or at least love him in her own way. They married just before she turned 18. The wedding was quickly put together and Suzie just went through the motions. She had no idea why, but the morning after they got married, she called Sammie's house. One of the boys answered and told her he was at work. She made him promise not to tell him that she called. What the hell was she doing?

With her fate sealed she went on to make her own little family. She stopped going to Berkeley, she just didn't care anymore. When she started feeling this baby move, her thoughts were always on Jonathan. She kept thinking that this entire past two years had been a nightmare and she would wake up one day and it would all just go away. Well, not so. She resigned herself to her future and moved through all the motions that were expected of her. She remembered her promise that if she had ever had a family she would do whatever it would take to keep them together and that is exactly what she did.

A few months later, Stan and Suzie moved to an apartment in town where Stan had become a police officer. He was working one evening, their daughter was asleep and Suzie went to take a shower. When she came out of the restroom, she found Sammie sitting in her living room. He looked terrible. Her heart skipped a beat and she was shocked. She asked him what he was doing there and he told her that he had come to see his daughter. What?

Apparently he had been keeping tabs on her and was convinced that Suzie's baby was his. She told him that the baby was not his daughter, she was born in August and they were together for the last time in November. She asked what he was doing there and he told her that he still missed her so much, loved her more than anything in the world and always would. He asked if she wanted to go with him, he would help her get a divorce and they could be together. He even offered to raise her daughter as his own. Suzie looked at him with a heart so heavy that all the memories came flooding back at her. She shook her head no, as much as she loved him she couldn't risk him hitting her again especially now that she had someone she had to take care of.

Sammie looked at her and with a choked voice softly told her,

"I will always remember you, especially the endless summer that is gone. I will be so lonely remembering you. I will never forget your sweet laughter the mornings after and your voice that was as soft as a summer breeze. Every time I look to the sky I will remember every bright star we made wishes upon. I will love you forever and I hope you will remember too. Suzie, I love you."

Suzie stood there stunned. Tears had started falling down her face and very quietly she promised him that she would remember too. Sammie wanted to kiss her, wanted to scoop her up and take her with him. When he made a move toward her, she stepped back and shook her head no. With that he was gone. She watched as he walked out of her life

A couple of days later, Suzie does not know why but she could not let go of him. She took her daughter and drove up to his house. Or, what used to be his house, someone else was now living in the house and they were gone. He was gone and she knew forever.

I will remember you.

Epilogue

How could I forget you? This book was derived from a diary I kept as a young girl. All of the events of this story actually occurred. While I was writing this book, I experienced a wide variety of emotions. One was remembering the love I was shown at a time when I desperately needed to learn that concept along with learning how to trust. Other feelings were of happiness, sadness, hurt, and terror. How one person can affect someone's life so intensely amazes me. One thing I can say for sure is this, I honestly believe that I felt a great and intense love for this man. Even after all he had done to me, our son and us, I carry that love with me even to this day. I only wish he had remained the person I once knew. Unfortunately he also took away the trust he had taught me. To this day I have serious issues with trusting anyone, including myself. So sad.

After 45 years, I learned the horrible truth. He had promised me that he would not drink again. Unfortunately, this proved to be a lie. He not only drank excessively, but he seriously abused and neglected the two boys, now men, that I had so easily come to love. When I learned this and was given detailed stories about their life after me, my heart broke. Not only for them, but for him. He missed out on the unconditional love of his children and that is sad for him. Those two boys missed out on having a loving parent, a good example and the laughter I used to hear on occasion. I now know why they did not laugh that often. It saddened me tremendously when I was told that they looked at me as their "savior from the beast." My heart still breaks for them.

I did forge ahead with my life and raise three incredible children. I did stay with Stan until all of the children were adults as I had promised myself all those years ago. Some say I should not have done that and we were not good for each other. Well, the past is the past and I will say this, in my own way I did manage to have some feelings for Stan. They certainly were never as intense as the feelings I had for Sammie, I will never allow myself to feel that way again. My children are now adults with lives of their own and each have reached their own pinnacle of success. I have also been blessed with two of the most wonderful granddaughters you could ever imagine. They certainly reminded me just how much you could love someone. I am so proud of those two girls and will cherish them for as long as I live and beyond.

I carry with me to this day the memory of Jonathan. I never had the opportunity to hear his voice or his cry, but I felt him move, I felt his life and I held him as his little body turned cold. He was my son. Everyone feels the loss of a loved one in different ways and whether it is a partner, a parent, a child or a child who never had the chance to live his life, it is a profound loss. I have never gotten over that loss but I have learned to live with it. He was precious. I used to think when my children were 17 how grateful I was that they never had to experience what I had at that age. I thank God for that blessing all the time.

During the course of my life, I sometimes wonder how things would have been if I had made a different choice and tried to stay to work through all the hurt with Sammie. His two sons assure me it would have been devastating. Something we will never really know for sure, it was a life time ago. I guess I will forever be curious. I just know one thing for sure, the love I felt for Sam and Teddy was genuine. I adored being around those two and to them I say I am so sorry for what you went through. I know you have grown into fine men and that warms my heart. Just remember, I loved you both.

The biggest question I came away from this whole process was wondering if Sammie every thought of me or our son again. I never doubted his love for me or at least the love he was capable of showing me. Alcohol can have a serious effect on one's person, both physically and mentally. All I know is how he treated me, the things he said to me, and the actions he showed. I never doubted he loved me and I know that I loved him with that once in a lifetime passion one rarely finds. I will always remember you.

Made in the USA
San Bernardino, CA
16 May 2015